CAPITAL GAINS

VT Bassett

Living Green Enterprises Inc.
902 – 5 Rosehill Avenue
Toronto, ON M4T 3A6

info@living-green.ca

First Living Green soft cover book edition 2010

This book is a work of fiction. Some places, marques and institutions are necessarily real to add context and authenticity. However, all names, characters, incidents, timing, procedures and methods of functioning are the products of the author's imagination or are used fictitiously. Any resemblance to actual events or persons is entirely coincidental.

Edited by Penney Alldredge in conjunction with Mike Drach.

Cover designed by SMB Freelance Design

ISBN-13 / EAN-13 978-0-9866944-1-7
ISBN-10 098669441x

For Debbie, Scott and Matt.

CAPITAL GAINS

PART ONE : INSIDER TRADING

CHAPTERS

Cherry Picking
Bearish Sentiments
Risk & Reward
Pump & Dump
Profit Taking

Cherry Picking

The Fat Guy stopped mid-sentence, turned to me and ordered in a rush. He then impatiently glared at his lunch companion, prompting him to hurry. The Fat Guy was anxious to tell his tale. He was a player. This was not to be missed.

I slalomed through the tables to the ordering hatch and shouted the order at Simon, head chef and fellow information thief. Then, I reappeared at the empty table nearest the Fat Guy and hovered around, fussing with linen, cutlery and glasses while tuning in as best I could to the story. It sounded like a winner.

"Wolf is managed by bastards," his companion was saying, "but I don't see them pulling the plug on this, it's too big."

"The geological report is crap. Plus, they couldn't stay in even if they wanted to; their board credibility has already tanked over that Alberta business," said the Fat Guy, buttering a bread roll. "But here's the thing," he continued, "when they get their stake back from this venture, where do you think they'll invest it next? Where are the world's best copper prospects?"

"Chile?" asked the other guy.

"Yup, Punto Lanza."

"You sure?"

"Positive. For one thing it's already producing," counted the Fat Guy on his stubby fingers. "Two, it's accessible, three, it's got a well-connected partner invested, four, it's got that massive option right next door, and best of all, I heard from a friend over at Personnel Security Services that they're getting ready to guard a bunch of new Wolf mining people in northern Chile."

"Sounds interesting."

"You bet. My theory is they've drilled a few holes into the Chilean option land, came up with some eye-popping grades, then got their geologists in Quebec to play down their local Chinese JV, so that they could extricate and put the cash into Chile."

The rest of their conversation, what snatches I heard, had drifted into the usual generalities (the economy, hockey, the kids). My zone filled up. I cruised around on the hunt for more info but what remained of that lunch session was largely unproductive.

Tobacco Road was a gold mine for its owner. The location was fantastic, right in the middle of Toronto's financial district. The restaurant did only two things: lunch and occasionally, private dinners. They did both very well.

It was great for us staff, too, because we didn't have to work every night. We basically got in at eleven in the morning and were done by 4:00 p.m. Lunch was always booked solid, always many days in advance. I had never seen a walk-in get seated; it was just that kind of place.

My patch was the primest in the place. Tables eight to eleven ran inside and parallel with booths twelve to fifteen, the only string of booths in the restaurant. Collectively, these eight dining clusters made up the Green Zone. The Green Zone was mine. I'd had to wait tables at the Tobacco Road for seven months to rise to a position that allowed me to claim this action. The Toronto Star had justifiably listed this as the hottest lunch spot on Bay Street. Within Tobacco Road, the Green Zone was the envy of the entire restaurant crew.

The afternoon passed quickly enough and before long, Simon was pulling on his Leafs jacket and eye-sweeping me to the door. I joined him outside. It was pissing wet, so I was pleased to be wearing my waterproof Aussie bush hat as we strode out together towards our shared apartment at College and Spadina.

"What you got?" I asked him.

"Rib-eye," he informed me rather proudly. This is how we ate. The boss didn't seem to check the actual inventory. He was a money kind of guy – revenue, costs, profit. How it came didn't really appear to worry him. He probably factored in a certain level of shrinkage, which was probably factored accordingly into our wage rate. The boss was a tough guy. We made sure to keep on the right side of him. Simon was always careful not to get caught slipping meat into that special inside pocket in his Leafs jacket. "What about you?" he asked.

I told him the Wolf story on the way back home and I sensed his interest. We liked mining stocks, especially the juniors. They tended to jump wildly on news, or rumors of news, or whatever. This sounded like a mining play to us, so we were anxious to get back to crime central to do some digging of our own.

Crime central was the middle apartment in a three story walk-up. It was right on the Chinatown side of the university, so the demographics were fairly predictable. Upstairs were three girls and downstairs were two boys, all of them students and all of them Chinese. They got together occasionally to eat, and that was always a noisy business, but for the most part they were studious and fairly quiet. The girls twittered and giggled whenever they saw us. We figured out a while ago that they suspected we were gay. We had resolved to prove them wrong, but thus far the opportunity had evaded us.

Simon opened the door. Quite a process in this neighborhood since we had three front door locks to get through. As we walked in past the kitchen counter, Simon slapped the steaks down and said "OK, let's see what we got," which is easily one of his favorite phrases. I got used to him muttering that to himself when we shared digs in Vancouver, while we were in business school together.

We both came out of that with MBAs the previous year. The recession had made it impossible to find a job in Vancouver so we headed to Toronto. Our timing could not have been worse, regardless of where we had decided to look. The recession was blowing in lusty and cold, and although the economic bottom had supposedly been reached, the smart money was still laying low. Investments, development and hiring were all in abeyance. The country was waiting this out. We were in our fifth month of job searching in Toronto and we needed work. Then we got lucky.

It was on our way to see another Bay Street recruitment firm that we walked past the Tobacco Road restaurant. A pale yellow handwritten sign declared that they were hiring. We noted this, but it took us few steps before we both stopped, turned around and looked again, this time actually seeing what was there.

"We don't see many of those," observed Simon, referring to the sign in the window.

"We have to pay the rent," I offered. "This'll be temporary, let's go check it out."

The boss met us on the floor. This would be the only time that I ever saw him with a broom in his hand. He wasn't happy about it either. "You guys looking for work?" he grunted between sweeps. Then he saw our suits and laughed, covering up his embarrassment. "We're not open yet," he said. "Give me a few minutes and I'll get the book," referring to the famous reservations book, although it meant nothing to us at the time.

"Actually, yeah," I said. "You were right the first time. We sure are looking for work. What work do you need doing?"

"I need a waiter and a line chef," said the boss, now looking a bit skeptical, still focused on my attire. "You guys got any experience in that area?"

"Sure," confirmed Simon, confidence oozing. His lightly freckled face and reddish hair combined to give him a friendly, trustworthy appearance. And with his muscular build, he looked like he could handle hard work. My dark hair on my wiry frame conferred no such advantages. I gulped, but Simon continued smoothly, "I'm the cook and Eric here waits tables."

"Where have you worked before?" the boss quizzed Simon. "You bring your references?" His eyes had narrowed and were probing us both. I was already anxious under the sudden spot-light. Like most university students we had worked our way around Vancouver, but few employers would remember us, let alone provide us with references. We were simply part of the available student pool who were willing to put in the hours for minimum wage.

Simon rattled off the names of a few of the better known restaurants. "And you have actually cooked for these establishments?" asked the boss. "Where are they?"

"Yes, part time. They're in Vancouver. We were studying there," Simon explained.

"And we don't have references," I said, a little forlornly.

The boss stared hard, thinking. "You're not making it very easy for anyone to employ you, are you?" he said. Then quite suddenly he grabbed my hand, pumped it once and said "OK, I'll try you guys out. Only because I'm in a bit of a hurry, my best waitress just ran off with the line cook." He seemed surprised that this could have even happened. "But you are on trial. Show me that you can do this properly and we will take it to the next level." We happily agreed.

We were taken to the staff room, shown a couple of spare lockers and each issued with a Tobacco Road shirt. Mine - waiter black; Simon's - chef white. "You'll get another one tomorrow," said the boss. "If you pass muster. So, let's go learn the menu," which started our foray into the service industry.

That was nearly 18 months ago.

Now, entering our living room, we headed over to Sherlock, our big desktop computer. "Let's check what Wolf Copper Resources is up to first," I suggested, taking control of the keyboard and mouse. Simon nodded in assent. "The Fat Guy made it sound like the poor geological report was coming from a prospect in Quebec."

"Their quarterlies should say something about this," Simon said. "Yup, over there," he pointed then leaned over to read the screen. Sure enough, our research showed that Wolf and a Chinese consortium had formed a joint venture partnership. The JV intended to develop the Quebec property into a copper mine, subject to the ore deposit being proven through a series of exploratory boreholes. These would be drilled by Wolf and paid for by the Chinese. Wolf had significant funds tied up in escrow against the joint development of this mine. The latest quarterly report declared that exploration results were anticipated in the next few months.

So far, so good. We navigated around a bit more and found the link to the Chilean mine, part owned by COBRECO, Chile's state owned copper mining company. There was a map of the region showing the extent of the Punto Lanza lease holdings, together with a large adjacent option. "Well, well, looks like you heard right," approved Simon. "Now the big question is whether or not these guys really are onto something down there."

We pulled up the corporate info. Punto Lanza was listed on the Toronto Stock Exchange with 30 million shares in issue. It was held 40 percent each by COBRECO and Wolf Resources, with the remaining 20 percent (six million shares) on the open market. We discovered that Punto Lanza was indeed prospecting their next door option, but so far no results had been reported.

TSE prelisting and reporting requirements made it fairly easy to get detailed information on most listed companies. Trading data is also available. It's all there in the TMX website. We looked at the trading activity – nothing special presented itself. Trading volumes were in a fairly predictable volume band around 10,000 shares daily and the price had remained in a range between $29.50 and $32.50 per share for the last three months. "OK, there's either nothing here, or we're the first to hear about it," I told Simon. He agreed. "So let's set up a tripwire, shall we?" I suggested, smiling.

In the land of insider trading, it was difficult to know who had the same information as you did. The best way to assess this was to watch the stock. If the information was good, something would start to happen to the share price or the trading volume, or most likely, both. Simon and I had written a simple program on Sherlock that took stock exchange data and statistically compared it against limits that we would set up for that particular stock. This worked a bit like the control limits on a statistical quality control system. If the price breached a particular limit (our tripwire), an exception report was generated.

Most stock exchanges refresh their Internet data every 20 minutes, which was plenty good enough for our purposes. But this did mean that a tripwire could be triggered at any time during the business day. So we needed to find a way that we could be alerted to this. This was accomplished by linking Sherlock to a simple GSM sender device we'd picked up in Chinatown. A GSM sender is essentially a stripped down cellular phone that transmits data over the local GSM cellular network. It needed it's own SIM card and some programming, but any time the tripwire was triggered, we got a text message from the sender directly to my cellphone. It showed the stock ticker symbol, the price and volume transacted.

This was good enough for us to decide whether or not to take a punt on the stock. The trick to this was to set the tripwire finely enough so that we could make maximum gains, but not so fine as to be triggered in the course of normal daily price and volume variations.

Over time, we became quite good at this and made a lot of money. Sadly, some of our earlier discoveries went completely untapped. We didn't have the money back then to make the stock bets, so we watched helplessly as the stock took off, or dived, depending on the information we had overheard. It was only when we took a final draw down on our student loans that we came up with the seed capital to try this out for real. Our stock broker took the money, opened an account for us in the name of our newly created BC Investment Club, and gave us his number to call.

We called the broker within the week, after overhearing an excited staffer describe how the Ontario government were going to roll out their impending green energy plan. We placed our entire $2,000 on a newly listed Ontario solar cell manufacturer and held our breath. A week later the Ontario government announced its new green energy policy, the solar company stock went through the roof and we made $11,000. The BCIC broking account presently contained a portfolio balance of $790,000 and we had long ago become addicted to the game.

An old adage maintained that eavesdroppers seldom heard anything good of themselves. As true as this might have been, it seemed to us that there was no shortage of secret commercial matter under discussion at the Tobacco Road. A smart man could profit from this. So it was to our great fortune that Toronto's business people clambered to get into the Green Zone booths. And in the Green Zone, my patch, I waited and I listened.

Bearish Sentiments

"Eric, wake up!" It was Simon shaking me awake at 10:00 a.m. "Punto Lanza is making a move, come check this out."

I forced my eyes open against the morning brightness, got out of bed and made my way over to Sherlock. Sure enough, Punto Lanza stock had started moving. It looked as if the volume would end up well over the 10,000 share daily average. "Something's up," I mumbled, redundantly. Simon knew that already.

"The price is still $33," said Simon. "Lets get in!"

"OK, how much do you want to go?" I asked. "5,000 shares? That's $165,000."

"Yeah, let's do 5,000," Simon said, magnanimously. We'd never bet that big before, our previous record was just over $100,000. Neither of us felt concerned though, this was a system with which we'd grown very comfortable. I placed the required orders with the broker then showered and got ready for a day at Tobacco Road. Or, as we had begun calling it, The Office.

Our first stop on the road to The Office was the Starbucks near the university entrance on College Street. It was a modest luxury we allowed ourselves now that we were seeing some success. We'd previously made our own coffee at the apartment. Then we got employed and we shifted to Tim Hortons. Now? Well, we'd become accustomed to the lattes at the top of the food chain. We knew that it was wrong, because if we had to pay for our food like normal people, we probably wouldn't be able to afford these. Despite the guilt, it was hard not to feel good about this habit, particularly when the barrista knew what we wanted as we walked through the door.

"Have you thought about when we should stop?" I asked Simon when we got back out onto College Street. He looked at me strangely and shook his head.

"Why would we stop?" he wanted to know.

"Well, insider trading is illegal, for a start," I responded. "They've developed all sorts of software these days to track big gains placed suspiciously close to a major share movement. You know this, Simon, don't be coy."

"Yeah, I know, Eric. I just don't want to stop before we hit a million," said Simon. Between the two of us, he was the greater risk-taker.

"Well, that's probably going to happen on this play. Are we ready to quit after that?" I wanted to know.

"Yeah, let the million happen, I'll be ready. You?"

"Ready. I'm already suffering a bad case of austerity fatigue and I want to do some spending." We both laughed.

"Hey, should we actually quit the office job?" asked Simon, suddenly excited. "How about we tell the boss today that this is our last day?" We laughed even louder. "Seriously, let's do it! Today!" Simon was quite animated. I found it hard to deflate the moment. It was too easy to stay caught up in the thrill of a momentous decision.

"OK, but let's wait until the end of the shift, I would hate the boss to have an avoidable coronary." I said and we both laughed again.

We got to the office on time. I don't think we'd ever been late,

come to think of it. Aside from stealing meat, we'd otherwise
worked hard to avoid conflicts, stay below the radar and
camouflage our real selves as best as possible. The prospect of
being free of this charade was now most welcome. I felt that
Simon shared the feeling too, even though we didn't vocalize it.
The boss greeted us warmly enough as we walked in.

I took a peek at the Green Zone bookings for the day. I didn't
recognize any of the famous captains of Canadian industry, but
then again, this part of town was all about stocks, bonds and
their many derivatives. The people in the know were not so
well known to outsiders like me. It could be refreshingly
inconspicuous. A research analyst could publish a report, hear
it being discussed by people at the next table and neither party
would know the other.

That day was like so many others before it, except I felt a little
sad to be leaving. We had developed a good rapport with the
other staff and I knew I would miss them. Yet there remained
the exciting tingle of finally quitting and getting on with life. I
could do a lot with my half million dollars and was certainly
thinking pleasantly along those lines when the guy sitting alone
at booth twelve stopped me cold.

"You guys are doing well, aren't you?" he said.

"Uh, excuse me?" was my confused response.

"Financially."

"Oh, uh, sure, the restaurant does well," I managed.

"I don't mean the restaurant, I mean you and your partner." His
tone had become a little flatter, more accusatory. I didn't like
this at all.

"I'm not a partner in this business," I said with a forced laugh, playing dumb.

"I know," the man said menacingly. "And you know what I'm talking about." He stared hard at me for a while, then suddenly got up, placed the bill folder in my hand and walked out the door. His bill was $26, but in the folder was a single $5 note. I felt light headed and I could physically feel the blood leaving my face. What the hell was this?

I went over to the serving hatch, beyond which I could see Simon in the kitchen grinning from ear to ear. He was obviously enjoying his last shift. He looked up at me, grin turning to concern and said, "Are you okay, Eric? You look terrible. Are you sick? Get the boss over here." He started poking his head and arm through the hatch to signal the boss over. I recovered fast.

"No! We've been busted," I managed to get out, simultaneously shoving Simon's arm back through the hatch. He started going the same color as me and I could see his legs buckle just a little.

"What? When? How?" he asked, each word separated by an increasingly nervous pause.

"We need to chat, but later. I'm not sure we should quit this job just yet either."

"What's the tea party about, girls," came the boss's gibe from behind me. "We have hungry people to feed." This was his standard line, but now he stopped suddenly and asked "What is it? You both look like shit. What's going on?"

I forced a recovery, but it was difficult. "Everything's fine boss, we're feeding them," I told him. It was the response he usually liked but in this case I could see that our collective state of agitation had made him suspicious. We both turned back to duty before the conversation got any deeper.

The rest of the afternoon went by with both Simon and I in assorted states of panic. The situation was aggravated by our inability to communicate, which might have somehow calmed me down. Instead, I found myself tuning in to different levels of random chatter from all over the Green Zone. I couldn't shut it out. I had developed this listening skill that had served us so well, but today it was a distraction that I seriously did not need.

Risk & Reward

We got home that afternoon without any food, so for the first time in ages we had to go out again and actually buy some. The rain had stopped and Toronto was looking slick in the low angle evening sunshine. We settled on a pre-cooked chicken from Sobey's and made our way home again. We had talked non-stop about the sinister man from booth twelve and try as we might, we just could not figure it all out. We eventually reduced our theories to a short list on Sherlock:

1. He's an investigator type, probably alerted to our investing success and is now suspicious.
2. He'd mistaken us for someone else.
3. He's a shakedown artist who somehow knows what we've done.

I had checked the reservations book during the shift and discovered that our friend had booked in under the name of Smith. Likely his real name? I didn't think so. Neither did Simon.

He had disappeared immediately so we had no idea where he had come from or where he was going to.

I didn't have a totally clear picture of this guy in my mind. My recollection was that he had dark hair, slightly graying near his ears. He was white. He might have been in his 40s or even 50s. He was of average height, average build and didn't sound foreign. He'd ordered steak and iced tea. He had only paid me $5. The tip? Anyway, I had still needed to cover his $26, so technically, I had just bought my tormentor lunch. This felt like a school yard bullying and it had left me feeling similarly unsettled.

"I hate to admit it," sighed Simon, rubbing his eyes. "But I can't shake the idea that we're dealing with an investigator. I just don't get this guy's strategy, though. If he had the goods on us, why not make an arrest, or whatever they do? Is this shock tactic supposed to scare us into doing something stupid? And if so, what?"

We sat there for a while longer, staring at Sherlock, waiting for an answer to pop out of the screen. "You know, it might be that they're suspicious but can't prove anything," I offered. "I mean, we've been careful."

Simon nodded. He knew that we had tried to cover our trades by letting the investments ride until we were ready to buy into the next one. Only then would we sell something to raise the money for the next buy. We had hoped that this delayed sell disguised our pattern of buying just before any sudden jump in stock price. Also in our favor was that we had started this venture at somewhere close to historic market lows. So, just having some skin in the game since the market bottom would have given us a nice profit ride in the subsequent recovery.

"Yes, I'd like to believe that it's difficult to prosecute these cases," he said. "Maybe we'll get lucky. So the obvious question now is what we should do to stay out of trouble."

"Assuming we're not already in it."

"Right."

"OK, then I think we should sell up and cash out," I suggested. "Which reminds me, we haven't even checked our portfolio." I pulled up the spreadsheet. We had it set up so that the latest closing prices automatically populated the spreadsheet at the end of each trading day. Today our total was sitting at $775,000 which was down $15,000 thanks to Punto Lanza having dropped $3 during the day.

"I wasn't expecting them to drop like that," said Simon. We looked a little closer and found that the volumes were up, 30,000 shares traded today. "OK, let's see what we got." Simon grabbed the mouse and hunted around all the news-wires to see if anything had broken on Punto Lanza that would justify today's action. Nada. No search hits at all.

"Maybe a private arrangement book-over?" I suggested. Simon renewed his vigor with the mouse and then whistled.

"Look at this!" he said excitedly, "According to this SEDAR record, Wolf made a book-over deal with COBRECO for 30,000 shares at $30. That was the only trade of the day! Wolf now have 40.1 percent. This sounds like a change of control to me."

"Well, well, something smells fishy in the state of Chile," I chimed in. "What does one partner know that the other of them doesn't?"

"Exactly!"

We were feeling energized now. Something was going down and we thought we knew what that was. It looked like Wolf had prior knowledge of the geological state of the option and had somehow convinced COBRECO to surrender joint control. COBRECO must clearly not have known what was really going on.

"Where are the Fat Guy and his friend in this?" I wondered. "Why aren't they part of this action?"

"If the friend reads SEDAR stuff, then there'll be fireworks tomorrow. We should try get some more Punto Lanzas first thing before they get too expensive," Simon suggested.

"Are you high?" I asked, incredulous. "This activity burst is exactly what we need to disguise our way out. Think about it, we move out and the share takes off. Who's going to suspect an insider trade with that logic? We've been given a neat escape here." I was really amazed that Simon saw this situation differently. It would be suicidal to go anywhere near another punt in my view. Just asking for trouble.

Maybe it was the relief of discussing something other than the Bogeyman from booth twelve, but for some reason we hooked into this new twist in the Punto Lanza story and just could not let it go. We speculated endlessly on what the price would do if they did hit good exploration grades. In the end, we thought it should at least double, consistent with a doubling of the size of the deposit. That made some sense. By this time, we had cracked open the bottle of red wine that the boss had gifted me a while back. It was corked, smelling a little of newspaper, but it still helped to lift the mood. We started to feel less vulnerable, convincing ourselves that catching insider traders was a lot more difficult than it seemed. The Bogeyman had started to look very much less scary.

Much later, we resolved to double the bet on Punto Lanza in the morning, provided of course that the market had not gone frothy with excess buyers before we could get in.

Pump & Dump

At exactly 9:15 a.m. the following morning I called our broker and gave him an order for another 10,000 Punto Lanzas "at best below $32". We received an email just before we left for The Office confirming the trade. He had secured us 10,000 shares at $31 each. We were ecstatic.

After getting in to Tobacco Road, I checked the lunch reservations for the Green Zone and found no Mr. Smith. Nor were their any other obvious false names, no Jones, no fairy tale characters, everything seemed normal. Then my hand started to shake at the entry for booth 14. Someone had made a booking for Wolf for four people.

I stayed agitated until the lunchtime trade started coming in. I desperately wanted to know who the booth 14 patrons were, but at the same time, I was as nervous as hell that it would be the Bogeyman again, perhaps this time with three giant policemen. I was playing with a rather inelegant exit, if that sequence of events unfolded, when the boss called me over to the front door. "Booth 14, for four," he told me, handing me four menus and herding the four diners toward me.

I leaned over to look at the book, pretending to see the name for the first time, "Mr. Wolf?" I asked enquiringly of the four of them.

"Wolf Copper, actually," one of them admitted. OK, that was a relief, I thought to myself. It also meant that a potential danger had just become an opportunity. I was smiling as I guided them towards both their booth and to the expensive wines on the back page of the menu.

They didn't order any wine, but then they didn't need to. They were clearly celebrating something. I caught a few references to the "poor Chinese" and whenever I approached the table they fell silent. A good sign in my book. Then, at the end of the meal, the guy who looked like the leader of this crew lifted his coffee cup and made a toast that I couldn't hear. "To Punto Lanza!" the rest of them chorused. Well that was it then, right?

Right!

Simon and I came back from the office, turned on Sherlock, and opened the spreadsheet to a very welcome $845,000. The Punto Lanzas had gone up eleven percent to $34.50. Turnover of Punto Lanza was 60,000 shares for the day. Perhaps the Fat Guy and his friend were getting in now. The rest of our portfolio had ticked up a little too. This was looking good.

We reasoned that if Wolf were being as underhand as we suspected, then it was unlikely they would release any exploration reports on the option property for at least a month. There needed to be sufficient time between their buying control from COBRECO and their announcing a great new development prospect. Anything else, we believed, would raise their partners' suspicions. We guessed that they might even release something negative first, just to make COBRECO feel good about their 39.9 percent decision. Well, that was theory, anyway, so we settled in to wait this one out.

The next day was a Friday, which was usually a big day at the office. The boss always tried to capitalize on the long lunch syndrome. Let's face it, he couldn't have packed another body into Tobacco Road using a crowbar, so the least he could do was to try to keep everyone there for as long as possible. This typically involved alcohol and I generally fluffed it up for all I was worth. My tips on a Friday were always excellent and easily justified the week's Starbucks habit.

As I cruised between tables with a good bottle of Porto and

offered shots to the customers, I started to hear chatter about Wolf, and more disturbingly, about Chile and copper. I could swear I had heard Punto Lanza mentioned at one table. It took me a while to notice that most of the patrons had turned toward the flat-screens hung judiciously here and there around the restaurant. The story of the moment was Punto Lanza. They had just announced a significant discovery on their option property and this, according to MSNBC, was set to redefine the copper landscape. Some journalistic exaggeration, perhaps, but the share price had already responded by jumping 20 percent and all of the people interviewed could only see more upside potential.

I caught some of the patrons taking discreet notes; some were even making calls. My guess was that the afternoon trading session at the TSX was going to be mighty interesting! I poked my head through the serving hatch to report this news to Simon. It was a good feeling.

The boss finally presented the last bill to the last table as the Friday fun wound down at about 4:00 p.m. People had few qualms about cavorting out of the office all afternoon, but they were suddenly very serious about getting home to the suburbs and not wasting their Friday evening in the traffic. We cleaned the place up, grabbed a few steaks for the weekend, and headed home ourselves. A quick check on Sherlock revealed that the Punto Lanzas had closed up nearly 40 percent to $48 per share. We were now sitting on a portfolio worth $1,047,500! We had become millionaires!

"Holy smokes!" I said, whacking the table, unable to contain myself and bursting into a laughing shout. Simon jumped up, pumping his fist laterally like a Stanley Cup winner. This was huge. Even Sherlock swayed happily on our rickety table.

After a few minutes of irrational exuberance, we calmed down, found chairs, and slumped quietly. The room was buzzing with silent thoughts, but we were too wired to muster them into coherent sentences. It was a lot easier just to go with the moment. Eventually, Simon made the only sensible suggestion. "Let's have a drink," he said. "I'm going down to the LCBO, you coming?"

The Liquor Control Board of Ontario maintained an outlet fifteen minutes away at the intersection of Dundas and Spadina. Even the homeless types hanging around outside couldn't cool our mood. We tore around the aisles with an undersized shopping cart and filled it to the brim with beer, wine and vodka. This was the first bit of opulent excess that we'd allowed ourselves since arriving in Toronto. For a couple of guys who liked good food and drink, we had been pretty restrained up to this point. The downside of letting our investments ride had been a constant need for party-thrift, so this made for a very welcome change. We were about to make a huge dent in our housekeeping fund; even more so when I threw in a packet of cigars at the till.

The walk home was tougher, carrying all that hooch. Despite this, we still managed two stops, the convenience store for some snacks, and Wei Fang for Chinese food. We got back at the same time as our various neighbors. The Chinese boys were chatting to the Chinese girls and they were all carrying books or backpacks.

"Hey, you guys want to join us for a drink?" I asked.

"Sure," answered one of the girls, as she grabbed the Wei Fang packet from Simon and peeked inside. "We'll get some more food," she declared, handing it back. "See you in half an hour." She then said something in Chinese to her friends, then asked, "Okay?" looking at me again.

I responded, "Great, see you then."

Simon had always been the food guy. He was good at it and enjoyed it, so I left him to plate the snacks and the Chinese food. I moved some stuff around our apartment and put the wine and beer in the fridge. Then I started Sherlock up, made up a playlist and soon had some good music going.

Simon and I had lived together since our second year at the University of Victoria. We had been friendly enough at high school and had shared many of the same interests.

Simon had come from a Navy family. His Dad was serving at CFB Esquimalt where he was known to be a tough task master. Much of his discipline and focus was transferred to Simon, partly by way of genetics and partly by way of assertion. Simon's Mom had died ten years ago and his father never re-married.

My folks were both teachers. Mom taught mathematics and Dad geography. Being teachers, they were also somewhat predisposed to orderliness, but not fanatically so. There were generally books and periodicals lying around our house, which provided they were contributing to our education was considered okay.

Our fathers barely knew each other but they shared a deep passion – hockey. So it was not surprising that Simon and I found ourselves being pushed to the limit in that area. I was quick, but too light to be a serious contender. Simon was slower, but much stronger. He was also a useful fighter. He hated bullies and never hesitated to drop his gloves and square off to anyone pushing the smaller players around. Being one of the smaller guys myself, I was targeted relentlessly on the ice. A lot of the time my speed kept me clear of the big hits, but all too often I would get creamed. Then Simon would get steamed and the reaction was predictable.

Eventually, our Oak Bay hockey coach couldn't take any more. He kicked us both off the team for being too disruptive. Our joint dismissal was the catalyst that brought us closer together.

That's when we took up rugby and enjoyed a couple of seasons playing for James Bay. That was also when we first took up digs together. I had always marveled at how this tough tackling, mud smeared hard man could transform himself into a culinary virtuoso. He was born to wear an apron, but you would need to be a brave man to tell him that.

He did a great job of it tonight, too, impressing the neighbors who had all arrived together. It turned out that the guys downstairs were called Billy and Adam. Upstairs we had Eva, Joy and Kelsey. I had told one of them some time ago that we both worked in a restaurant. It wasn't exactly high-paying work, so I made up a story that we'd won some money today at the races and were celebrating.

"Horse racing?" asked Kelsey, eyes widening.

"Yeah," I answered, clueless.

"Waah, really?" she asked, getting animated. "What number?"

"Race eight, horse eight," I said, which really got her excited. It turned out that her father was a big shot in the Hong Kong Jockey Club and she was a major fan of horse racing. Of course, I had known that eight was a pretty lucky number amongst the Chinese and had thrown that in for its cultural value, but the combination of a lucky number, a noble endeavor, some good music, and a lot of alcohol got me lucky with Kelsey that night. We slipped away to my room where she jockeyed me like she was bringing it home in the Queens Plate at Woodbine. Any lingering doubts about my orientation should have disappeared after that performance.

It was one wild night, capping off a great day.

Profit Taking

It took the rest of the weekend to get the apartment back together again. Every now and again one of us would start to laugh, remembering something else that had happened on Friday night.

"Do you remember making beef with black bean sauce?" I asked at one point.

"Aw jeez, really?" asked Simon.

"You don't remember, do you?" I chided. "I came in here to get some water. You were cooking up all the steaks, no shirt, wearing some crazy headband, steam and smoke everywhere. Joy and Eva were down to their underwear, singing into their salad spoons, and you were all smoking cigars." There was plenty of humor with each new revelation.

We did see Adam and Billy at some point the next day. They had gotten blasted and left around midnight. Billy was looking profoundly unwell. The girls, however, just disappeared. We figured they didn't get up at all on Saturday, then went for some retail therapy on Sunday to cleanse the soul, heal the spirit and write the hymn-sheet for what they would say to us the next time we met.

On Sunday night, we got serious again. We had to figure out how best to cash out from the market, deposit our funds, quit our day jobs, and get on with the rest of our lives.

"I think we should call the broker first thing tomorrow and sell the portfolio," suggested Simon.

I agreed with this tactic. Then, I suggested that when we go to The Office tomorrow, we make that our last shift.

Simon nodded, suggesting, "Then after work we hightail it to the broker's office and pick up our check. There should still be enough time to make it to the bank and deposit this."

"Okay, but two checks would be better. I'll ask the broker," I said. "Do we need to give them a reason why we're closing the account?" I asked. Simon didn't think so. I wasn't so sure so I filed it away to come up with something plausible. I was feeling inexplicably nervous.

"What are you going to do with your money?" Simon asked, after a while. It was the first time we'd broached this subject and it was still tentative. We didn't want to jinx the situation, but it was hard not to think about it now that the money was so close to hand.

"I want to buy a condo and get a real job," I told him. "I want to be in a position where I really don't have to think about making rent payments or any of that. Where I can focus on a great career."

"Oh," I added, "I also want a boat and a Harley!" We laughed like that was the funniest scheme in the world.

When the frivolity passed, Simon said, "Well, I want a floatplane and I want to take a few months to get my license so I can fly the thing. Then I want to start up a floatplane business, nothing fancy, maybe fishing excursions or outpost resupply, something like that." After a while he turned to me and said, "If I threw in a boat and a Harley, would you consider coming in with me?"

I knew that this was a serious proposal and that it required a serious response, but it had caught me off-guard. I must have appeared a bit startled. Simon looked as if he was going to make a retraction, but before he got there I said "I wonder if we could get a boat big enough to live on and still afford to get a float plane and a couple of Harleys?"

He recovered quickly, "A couple of float planes!" he said, enthusiastically. "And yes, we can live on a houseboat; we'll figure something out!"

In truth, I had not given enough thought to our future. I had more or less concluded that separation was inevitable; once we cashed out, we would part ways. But when it came down to it, I was touched that Simon sought to include me in his venture. As usual, he had seen through to the core of the issue well before I had. We were good friends, had survived the lean times cheerfully, put in some tough hours together, and come through it. Why not continue? Let the investment in each other ride.

We had another late night, drinking left over wine and making plans for Saskwatch Airways, our temporary name for our new venture. At some point, we heard the girls tripping past on their way upstairs. They were making just enough noise to announce that they were home, but we ignored them all the same. We were on another roll.

The next morning, I got my head on straight and called the broker. I explained to the reception lady that we wanted to cash up. She sounded a little shocked and passed me on to Bruce, the partner responsible for our account.

"Mr. Hanson? This is Bruce James. I look after your portfolio. Sunee tells me that you wish to dissolve your investment club account. Is that correct, Mr. Hanson?" Bruce asked smoothly.

"Yes, Mr. James. My partner and I have decided to start up a company together and we're going to need those funds. Would you be able to liquidate our portfolio today?"

"All of it? Today?" repeated Bruce. It was a stockbrokers habit to confirm instructions, I guessed.

"Yes. We would really like to be able to collect the proceeds this afternoon," I told him. There was a silence on the other side. I heard some paper shuffling around and some keyboard strokes, then Bruce came back up.

"Right, well I see that your portfolio is running at just over a million. Okay. These sales will have to to clear before we can cut a check," Bruce informed me.

"How long will that take?" I asked him.

"Oh, I expect that you could collect it here on Friday. Alternatively, we could post it to your address," Bruce said, helpfully.

"We'll collect," I said. "And please make out equal checks to me and my partner, Simon Goode."

"Done. Sunee will call you when the checks are ready and she'll have them for you at the front desk. Thank you for your business, Mr. Hanson, and do come back to us when you're ready to make some more investments." He seemed like a nice guy.

Nevertheless, we were quite bummed out by this latest turn of events. Having never cashed out before, we hadn't known there would be a delay. On the positive side, though, it meant that we were in no great rush to leave the Tobacco Road today. The boss might appreciate our giving a week's notice.

The boss had grown up in Africa, but had eventually escaped the madness of trying to farm there as a privileged white person. He'd managed to get into Canada and had then worked his butt off to establish the Tobacco Road. This had been made easier for him because he had been managing people since he was six years old and considered himself an excellent people reader.

What he had read in us, he said, was that we were two bright but desperate young guys who had needed a break in the middle of the worst recession in modern times. He thought of us as Simon and Garfunkel, except physically we were the other way around. Simon's bigger than me, he explained irrelevantly. Anyway, he had given us a break. In return, he had seen how hard we worked and had appreciated that.

That attitude had gotten Simon promoted to head chef and was why I had been given the Green Zone when we both still so clearly lacked the experience. It was also why he had turned a blind eye to our taking all those steaks over the months. That had made us blush and stammer, but he waved it away. "Youngsters like you have to eat," he offered. "My wife would have had it no other way. At least this way I didn't have to keep inviting you over to make sure that you were healthy enough to work." We all laughed gratefully.

"So, I suppose you've finally found something equal to your talents?"

"Yes, boss, we've got what we want now, but really, none of it would have been possible without you. We're extremely grateful. Thank you." It was not enough, I knew, but the boss stood up and extended his hand.

"Cheers then Eric, Simon, thanks for your hard work and my best for your new life. I know you'll do well, and when you do, you come back here and spend a bit of money at the Tobacco Road, you hear?"

"Hey boss, what about the rest of the week? Do you need us?" asked Simon.

"Nah. I can see that your mind is somewhere else. Don't worry, I've been building a reserve bench and I've also got my eye on a couple of staff from nearby places. Some a lot better looking than you two," he chuckled.

He was a great guy. We owed him, big time.

~~~

PART TWO : BEAR SQUEEZE

CHAPTERS

Short Squeeze
Due Diligence
Beating the Street
Dividend Clawback
Change of Control
Fill or Kill Order
Whistle-blower
Green Shoots

Short Squeeze

Now that we had the time, we decided to take the girls out for dinner. We ambushed them on their way back from U of T and bullied them into a weird sort of three on two date. It was a lot of fun. We teased them about what had happened the other night, but we also talked a lot, getting to know them much better. We traded phone numbers.

When we got back to the apartment the three of them said goodnight to us on the steps. There was no suggestion of anyone staying the night where they shouldn't, which was just as well, because the next morning would have been awkwardly uncomfortable.

It started with a mighty crash at just after 5:30 a.m. that rattled my bedroom door and woke me up. Then my door was flung open and the Bogeyman from booth 12 the other day was in my doorway, demanding that I get the hell out of bed and onto the floor. Behind him were two uniformed policemen. Behind them, I could see Simon through the open doorway to his bedroom lying naked on the cold laminate floor. One of the cops had his pistol pointed at him. The other had his pointed at me. They looked mean and angry. I froze, but this was not what the Bogeyman wanted. The nearest cop lunged towards the bed, pulled the sheets off me, and yelled, to get the hell onto the floor. The cop behind him was shouting now as well. I rolled onto the floor as fast as I could.

The noise subsided, as if the Bogeyman had lifted his hands for silence. He walked forward. I could see his shiny shoes inches from my face.

"Are you Eric Hanson?" he asked at a much more reasonable volume.

"Y-Yes," I stammered, lip trembling. "Why?"

"Because I am arresting you and your accomplice, Simon Goode, for insider trading. Now get up and put some clothes on, both of you."

My spine went soft and my forehead hit the floor. Nothing good was going to come of this. I struggled to breathe.

"Now!" barked the Bogeyman. My spine stiffened enough to get up. I went in search of clothes. Despite my anxiety, I couldn't stop thinking about which outfit might be considered jailhouse appropriate.

Simon was in a daze when I saw him a few minutes later. We had both changed but not showered. Our hair was still sticking up at odd angles. He still had pillow marks on his face and his eyes were red.

The cops handcuffed us then hustled us down the stairs into a waiting cruiser. Its lights were flashing. People were staring at us, but I didn't think we knew any of them. We were feeling so sorry for ourselves that neither of us spoke the entire journey. To their credit, the two uniforms in charge of us didn't speak either. I stared blankly forward, right at their Ontario Provincial Police shoulder flashes.

After a fast 20-minute ride, we arrived at the OPP Detachment just north of the 401 on Keele. The uniforms parked their cruiser up against the building and waited, still soundless. It took a few minutes for the Bogeyman to drive up in a blue-gray Ford Crown Victoria. The uniforms got out and went over to the Crown Vic. They started talking to the Bogeyman while still keeping an eye on the two of us. I quickly turned to Simon and said, "Listen Simon, we might get split up and the last thing we need is to be caught up in a bunch of conflicting stories, okay?"

"I was thinking the same," said Simon. I don't think he was, he still looked shocked.

"So the best policy here is to tell the truth, okay, Simon?" I suggested.

"All of it?" he asked, now looking at me.

"Yes, all of it." I thought for a second. "Let's not volunteer info unnecessarily," I qualified for him. "But let's not lie about anything."

"Okay, let's not admit to any insider trading, either," he said. And with that, the Simon I knew was back. I flashed him a grateful smile.

"Exactly," I confirmed softly as the uniforms open our respective back doors. Having a plan felt like we'd armed up, albeit with the very lightest of ammo. But at least it was ammo.

The OPP guys steered us out of their cruiser and into the building. It was about 6:30 a.m. and the station was quiet. A few more uniformed cops were inside and they looked up at us from what they were doing. They didn't seem surprised or even interested in our case. Our two cops took us into an empty office. It looked as though it was used by visiting officials – everything was there and it was all set up, but it was completely devoid of any permanent clutter. There were three chairs facing the desk. One of the OPP guys pointed to these and commanded "Sit!" Like obedient puppies, we sat. The two of them spun around and left the office.

The door opened again even before it had a chance to properly shut behind the uniforms. The Bogeyman walked in, looked at us like we were dirt, and sat carefully on the other side of the desk. He fiddled around with his briefcase, pulled out a ring-bound notebook and scratched around for a pen. He lay these items down on the desk. Then his hand went back into the briefcase for a while and he came up with a slim digital recorder. This too went onto the desk. He looked up from arranging his stuff and stared at us for a full minute. His eyes bored into ours. He didn't seem to need to blink which made my eyes tear up unaccountably.

Then he sighed loudly and opened his notebook to an empty page, wrote today's date up in the top right corner, underlined it, looked at us again, then very carefully wrote our names on the top line of the page and underlined these, too. The impression I got was that he was hugely angry, but bottling it for the sake of our well-being. It was uncomfortable, to say the least.

He switched on his recorder, cleared his throat and, leaning slightly forward, addressed the machine. He announced the date, the time, and the OPP Detachment call-sign. "This is Detective Sergeant Parry of the Ontario Provincial Police, Anti Rackets Branch, currently assigned to the Insider Trading Unit of the Joint Securities Intelligence Unit of the Ontario Securities Commission." He paused, then looked up at us. It was apparent that this was as much of an introduction as we were going to get from him. "State your names and addresses for the record," he commanded us.

I started, "Eric Hanson, 2 Fontana Court, 470A Spadina Avenue, Toronto."

Simon followed, "Simon Goode, 2 Fontana Court also, Toronto."

"Thank you," Detective Sergeant Parry said, politely. "Now, please describe and explain the insider trading scheme you two have been conducting, which led to your arrest this morning. Mr Goode, you first."

Simon glanced over at me, lips pursed. Then he looked at Parry and said, "Detective Sergeant Parry, I'm not sure that what we did was wrong. We acted on information that we overheard at the Tobacco Road restaurant..." which was as far as he got.

"Please, Mr. Goode!" Parry said sarcastically, "you people have *knowingly* acted on *information in your possession* that has *not been generally disclosed* and has *significantly affected the market price* of various stocks on the TSE. That, my friend, constitutes insider trading. Your trading activity has been investigated by the Joint Securities Intelligence Unit and recorded pursuant to criminal proceedings. You two are in big trouble! The only question is how big. Clear?"

His emphasizing certain pieces of what he'd just stated sounded very legal and very serious. Parry looked serious. The whole damn business of being here was serious and it sounded as if we had just been seriously busted. So much for our parking-lot bravado; I was getting ready to fold.

Simon said "Are we entitled to lawyers?"

At which point, I thought Parry would implode. He looked murderously at Simon and hissed, "That is your right, yes, but I would urge you to think about it, carefully. If you lawyer up to frustrate the course of justice here, then we are heading for a whole new ball game. For one thing, I'm going to throw you straight into jail," he growled, pointing to some evil place beyond the corner behind him. "Then we'll see how long it takes for your lawyer to get you out of there. You wanna go down that route, son?" Parry glared at us some more.

As menacing as this sounded, it offered a very faint prick of hope. Did he just put a condition on throwing us into jail? Did this mean that we might not be going straight in after all? I wasn't sure that Simon had picked up on this nuance so I said to Parry, "As Simon said, Sir, we are just not sure that what we did was wrong. Can we at least talk about that?"

"Go on."

So I told him the whole story, emphasizing that we had acted on bits of information that we had picked up in passing and being careful not to admit guilt anywhere. He took some notes, but let me finish without interrupting. At the end of my spiel, he turned to Simon and asked "Anything to add, Mr. Goode?"

"No, that covers the situation," answered Simon.

"Fine," said Parry, switching off the recorder. He stashed it back in his briefcase and stood up. "You two stay right there," he ordered as he went out the door, closing it behind him. We looked at each other. Simon lifted his eyebrows at me expectantly until I explained to him why I had just caved in. Only then did he seem to relax a bit.

The door opened and a much younger uniformed cop brought in two coffees in thick ceramic excess-fathers-day-gift mugs and plonked them down on the desk. "These are for you," he told us and disappeared again. They tasted like home made double-doubles and were mighty welcome after our morning so far.

After half an hour, Detective Sergeant Parry returned and eased himself behind the desk and sat down. He rubbed his eyes tiredly then folded his arms and sat back in his chair. "My bosses want a conviction," he said. "On the face of it, you two are certainly chargeable, maybe even culpable. Pursuing a pair of white collar criminals through the courts would make my bosses very happy and you two qualify nicely. So, it looks like that's what we're going to do here, go for a conviction."

"Wait a minute, Detective," said Simon. His face began to slowly flush pink and the big vein running down his neck started to visibly pulse. I had seen these signs before - this was Simon becoming angry. "After what we've just told you," he continued, "you can't possibly believe that you have a serious case against us. You would be going after us merely to make some kind of political statement."

"You prepared to take that risk, son?" asked Perry softly. The quiet way he asked the question made it all the more menacing, and credible. I noticed that Simon's anger was giving way to uncertainty.

"Could Mr. Goode and I take a minute to talk privately, Detective?" I asked Parry. He stared at me a while, silently. Then, quite suddenly he stood up and made for the door.

"Two minutes." he said, curtly.

"Shit," I said after Parry had closed the door behind him. "We could be in trouble here. Any thoughts?"

"Yes, I'd like to strangle that bastard."

"Do you think we could offer to pay a fine?" I asked.

"How do you do that without admitting guilt?" Good question. We tried to thrash it out logically, but it sounded very weak, and very guilty.

Our time was up. Parry swung through the door, all business again. "Well?" he demanded, simultaneously sitting and nudging his briefcase out of the way with his foot. I wondered then if he'd left his recorder running in there while he was out. Best to stick to the truth in case.

"Look, Detective, we're pretty sure that we're innocent here but we really don't want to be dragged through the courts to prove it," I said. "Is there any other way that we could solve this?"

Parry's eyebrows arched as he looked at me, incredulously. I realized then that my last question had sounded suspiciously like a bribe and quickly moved to correct myself. "I mean, could we pay a fine? Could we put it down to our poor judgment or something?" I sounded a little desperate now.

Parry looked at me for a long time before he asked, "Would you be able to recognize the two men you overheard discussing Punto Lanza stock?" I was sure that I could and I told him this. "OK," he said. "The Ontario Securities Commission are prepared to do a little horse-trading from time to time, so here's the deal. You guys help us catch some heavy hitting tippers and, provided you agree never to trade securities in Ontario again, we'll excuse your recent shenanigans."

"Tippers?" I asked, a little confused. They hadn't tipped me that much.

"People who *knowingly convey inside information*, thus tipping selected people off to their advantage." Again, the legal emphasis. He did that quite well.

I looked at Simon. He shrugged. It seemed like a very reasonable trade. "Deal!" I said. Parry, expressionless, bent down to retrieve his briefcase and got up to leave.

"I'll need a few minutes," he said and left us alone again.

He was back fifteen minutes later, smelling of cigarette smoke. He hoisted his briefcase onto the desk, opened it and extracted two sheets of paper. He placed these on the desk in front of us. They seemed to be agreements. Our names were printed, one on each and the page contained a few clauses obligating us to assist the OSC in any way possible in order to bring the tippers to justice. It also stated that we agreed never to trade securities in Ontario again. Big deal.

Parry handed over his pen. "Sign," he said. "Then I can brief you."

We duly scanned through, signed and dated the agreements. I could see that Simon was just as relieved as I was as we handed the documents back across the desk. Parry pulled out an official looking rubber stamp from one of the desk drawers, inked it and banged it down on each document. Then he signed the documents somewhere within the newly stamped area and put these back into his briefcase.

Parry leaned back, hands clasped on top of his head. He took a deep breath and said, "We think that there's a criminal organization operating here in Toronto who somehow have their hooks into key people in certain listed companies. They induce them into giving up inside information. Then, the organization acts on this information, possibly by acquiring stock and possibly holding it in one of their associated companies, which they would do carefully, and well in advance. Then close to the event, they tip off various fund managers in town."

Parry looked at us to make sure we were following. We were. "This has a few effects. One, it pumps up the stock price, and two, the increased volume hides their own insider trading activities as they sell off."

Simon and I glanced at each other. This was a simple but effective scheme. We could appreciate why Parry might have thought that in us, he had busted someone in the organization. They had obviously also played the Punto Lanza stock.

He clarified one last thing, "I am the lead investigator on this case and you two will report to me. Clear?"

The younger cop who brought in the coffee gave us a ride

home in another cruiser. We were all just as silent on the ride
back as we had been on the way in.

Due Diligence

"Let's go get something to eat," I suggested to Simon once we were out of the cruiser. We headed off to the Tim Hortons close by and got into the early morning queue. Once we had coffee, a breakfast sandwich, and a place to sit down, I asked Simon what he had made of the morning's events.

"Well, frankly, I am incredibly happy that we didn't go to jail, but I think we've been manipulated," he allowed. "It seems pretty convenient to me that he had those contracts drawn up already."

"Wait, what do you mean 'already?'" I asked. "He drew them up when he left the office, didn't he? That's why they were so short and to the point, surely?"

"Wake up, Eric," said Simon sharply. "No bureaucrat could have written that up so fast. All he did was go outside for a smoke!"

"Ah, shit!" I said, realizing that he was absolutely right, we had been played for patsies here. "I'm sorry, I shouldn't have agreed with him so fast." I was distraught.

"That's okay. I only realized it myself in the cruiser coming home. I'm just pissed that neither of us saw it at the time. It's kind of obvious now."

"You know what this means though, right?" I said. "It's likely that they knew they couldn't prosecute us all along." Then when I thought about it some more, I added, "Which explains why Parry came to the restaurant to scare us. Why he put on such a big show with guns and cops today. He wanted us vulnerable enough to sign up to help him on this case."

"Yeah," said Simon. "Let's use this to learn something about

Parry. And also about how difficult it must be to prosecute these cases. We had to have been right about that the first time."

"Does this mean we get to keep the money?" I wondered. Simon thought that we had better not bring that up with Parry, which sounded like a sensible strategy.

We got back to Fontana Court and saw that our broken door was leaning precariously across the doorway. Inside everything appeared to be where we left it, including our cellphones. Simon's phone was blinking away and he retrieved three messages. The girls wanted to know what had happened and Joy told him that they closed our door. That last bit seemed superfluous given where we had spent the morning in relation to Simon's phone.

The next message was from Sunee at the stockbroker's to tell us that she had been informed that the OSC had confiscated our portfolio settlement proceeds and that she had been instructed to send the checks to the OSC when they were ready. She was sorry.

Fuck!

The last message was from Parry. He wanted us to meet him on the sidewalk at 11:00 a.m. sharp at 20 Queens Street West, downtown. Simon, usually slow to anger, suddenly hurled his cellphone down with massive force. It shattered magnificently, but somehow didn't even scratch the laminate floor.

There was a Home Hardware close by where we got some quick-setting epoxy resin for fixing the door-frame. We filled the original hinge holes with this stuff and screwed the door back into the frame. We shimmed it with a pair of door jams and locked it to let it dry in place while we each took a long overdue shower. It had been a hell of a day already.

Once cleaned up, we set off to find 20 Queens St. W. It took us 35 minutes to walk to the corner of Queen and Yonge, where we were surprised to see that number 20 was the Queen St. entrance to the Eaton Center. Who knew? Standing right outside, smoking, was Detective Sergeant Parry. He looked a little agitated because we were early and he hadn't finished his cigarette. So he sucked it down, stomped it out and headed inside. We followed him to a bank of elevators. He took us up to the 18th floor.

Stepping out, we were faced with a reception desk directly opposite the elevator bank. The wall behind the reception desk declared in big letters that we had entered OSC JSIU. The back wall was connected to the elevator wall by glass walls on either side, so that the desk sat alone inside this sterile area. Parry walked us up to the reception desk and introduced us to Mai See, explaining to her that we were the two who were working with him on that case. He had obviously pre-cleared us because she knew all about us and had even prepared access cards for us. We got in via a security chamber built into the one glass wall, which only allowed access to one person at a time. Parry sent us ahead. We waited on the other side, watching as he got past the first door, which closed as the second door opened to let him into the secure area beyond the glass wall.

"Right, welcome to the Joint Securities Intelligence Unit," he declared. "Quick orientation, toilets over there, coffee over here, your desks are these two here, my office is that one in the corner." In his economic fashion, Parry explained that the JSIU reported to the OSC, but that it was staffed by a mixture of RCMP detectives, mainly from the CCB and IMET, an Integrated Market Enforcement Team. It also included some OSC and IDA investigators and various other members of the OPS, like ACA's when required. He was the only police detective and was on assignment from the ECU, which was a part of the ARB as we might have heard earlier had we been paying attention. Clear?

It turned out that the JSIU was structured into a few units of its own. Parry ran the Insider Trading Unit and there were others, like the ominous sounding Boiler Room Unit, which conjured up images of people and documents being shoveled into a raging fire. Anyway, our only concern was to be the ITU, and within it, DS Parry.

Parry took us over to the electronic side of the business, which was really quite impressive. Analysts and investigators hunched over screens, looking at trading information from all of Ontario's securities houses and which involved equities, bonds, certain derivatives and a lot of other stuff in between. We were steered towards Mary, a young analyst who looked exclusively at data from the Toronto Stock Exchange (TSX), the senior equity market in Ontario and the largest by market value in Canada. Mary would be our link to the machine. Any electronic information that we needed, we were to ask Mary. We were assured that if it was possible, she would get it.

Next came the library and filing area. It was policed by an efficient looking guy called Mike. We didn't get his last name. Mike could find anything we needed that had ever appeared in the press or had ever been reported by any branch of the government, provincial or federal. Presumably, this impressive collection of newspapers, books and reports was in a database on his computer, because his computer was all he seemed to have.

There were other areas that we were told were off limits to peons like us.

At the end of the tour, Parry took us to his office. He had a big desk full of papers, connected to a round table pushed up against it. There were five chairs tucked in around the round table. DS Parry, it seemed, liked to conference. He motioned us toward the round table and we took a seat on either side of where it connected to his desk. Parry edged around his desk and sat down. He got straight to it. "Okay, gentlemen, the discharging of your debt to the OSC starts now."

He explained that there were some additional details to the case that they'd pieced together over the last year or so. He'd left that file in one of our desks. Glancing out toward the desks, he said "There isn't much there. I'm relying on you two to flesh this thing out. We have no idea which companies are being manipulated by the criminal organization, but we are pretty sure that this organization exists."

The organization had been whispered about in intelligence circles for a year or so, with few details known and from sources whose credibility was already compromised. Parry told us they were calling this organization "Alpha" for now. The plan was to build this case into something that they could go after legally and prosecute.

Parry explained his theory: "It seems to me that one way we can do this is to work backwards. Use the electronic history to highlight periods of sudden stock price movement, then see if we can link this movement to specific information that might have been known some time in advance. We'll need to exclude anything random that was clearly unforeseen, and also any act of God, like an earthquake. If we can check those two boxes, then we could look for share transactions bracketing this sort of event." So far, this made sense.

"But," he explained, "how long of a period we'd need to search before the event depends on how long somebody could have reasonably known about it." The next phase, Parry explained, would be to look for patterns in the execution of these trades. He told us that if we could start identifying people, companies, brokers and any other players, we'd begin building a picture of the entire operation.

Parry continued, "This is a lot of work, especially for someone unfamiliar with these sorts of things, which is where you two come in. You're smart, appropriately educated, and have actually been involved in exactly this sort of skulduggery. Which, incidentally, is exactly why you also owe the OSC your best efforts in this endeavor. Use a thief to catch a thief, eh?" Parry was pleased with himself. "So, take the rest of the day to familiarize yourselves with the case and to come up with a strategy to move this investigation forward. Clear?"

"Clear," we echoed. We were getting used to this guy. He was actually quite smart. It would have taken him three years to scope, motivate, budget, hire and train a couple of MBA graduates to do this kind of work. Here he was getting the two of us for nothing and assigning us an awful lot faster.

Simon and I found the JSIU file in his desk and got reading. There was pitifully little in the file, which seemed to have been put together by an OSC investigator by the name of Alan Summer. We resolved to find this character and see if he could tell us more. I went to ask Parry where we could locate him.

"Oh, right, I meant to tell you that Mr. Summer died in a road accident in Quebec six months ago," he said. Well, that put an abrupt end to our first official line of investigation.

So we spent the afternoon strategizing, which at times felt more like guessing. We began to understand that this was not going to be a quick assignment. It could take months.

By the next morning, we had finalized the statistical limits to sudden, unexplained stock price movements that could be considered an "episode" and, in keeping with the culture of the JSIU, we acronymed these to PEITs (Potential Episodes of Insider Trading). Mary loved that. She set off happily to program the machine to look for PEITs going back two years.

Next, we set out to highlight the Obvious Big Events (OBEs). These were events that might have had a bearing on any stock simply due to its significant nature, but which could not have reasonably been foreseen by Alpha. These would be the stock price moving events to be excluded in our analysis. We discovered that we had to do this by sector, since OBEs affecting mining stocks were not necessarily the same as those affecting tech stocks for example. This was going to take some time, even with Mike's valuable assistance.

We slugged it out day after day, isolating OBEs, sifting through Mary's newly titled PEIT Reports, and gradually built up the picture for Parry. On the second Friday afternoon, Parry called us to his desk to conference the events so far. Although it had been slow going, he seemed impressed with our progress. At the end of the meeting, he pulled a couple of envelopes out of his desk drawer and handed us one each. We could see through the transparent window that our names were printed on whatever was inside.

"They're your paychecks," advised DS Parry. "You don't think that we condone slave labor around here, do you?" That was a nice surprise. "And by the way," he continued, "you can bring me any reasonable expenses incurred in the course of your investigations, and take note please – no original receipt, no reimbursement – that's my simple rule."

The paychecks weren't a fortune, but they beat the minimum wage, paid the rent, bought the food, and even funded a few drinks here and there. We made sure, however, that the first claim Parry got from us was for the front door epoxy, a new cellphone for Simon, and the lunch I'd bought him at Tobacco Road.

We got paid for the epoxy.

Beating the Street

After another two weeks, Simon called over from his desk at the JSIU, "Hey, Eric. Come look at this." He had found an emerging pattern. "See, these three companies each had a PEIT and this fourth company had two. What's interesting is that they all share a common parent. What I'm thinking is that the information might be coming from within the holding company." I thought he was definitely onto something there. It would make so much more sense for Alpha to squeeze, or grease, one parent company exec than many daughter company execs.

We figured that at the very least, if we focused our efforts on related companies, we might be able to flesh out the canvas faster. I called Mary in and together we worked out the parameters necessary to start grouping the PEIT-afflicted companies into sibling clusters. Not all siblings are equal, which is especially true in the corporate sense, so we further differentiated them by common control.

It felt as though we were getting somewhere when we went to Parry's bi-weekly meeting late on Friday. He thought so too. "You see?" he said proudly, "I knew you were the right guys for the job!" He had an interesting insight too, suggesting, "Let's try to pick out which Funds are active in each of these PEITs. It might be that for whatever reason, certain Fund managers are being fed certain information, possibly related to the source, or the industry, or the type of information or something similar."

I felt oddly proud that Parry had started using our PEIT acronym as part of his OSC terminology. It immediately sounded so much more credible.

We got Mary onto this after the weekend. The trouble was that there were many, many Funds in town. This was starting to become a rather unwieldy matrix. We needed to dissect it into bite sized chunks. After all, as our Tobacco Road boss was fond of telling us, "You *can* eat the elephant, but only one bite at a time." So we got her to run a parallel search of market activity by major Fund. We could connect the dots later.

This Fund analysis turned out to be comparatively easy. Since we had the PEITs pegged, we could track an individual Fund's trading activity around that stock. We found that four large Funds and one small, recently formed Fund consistently triggered our statistical tripwires. We sensed that we had isolated the 80 percent pool of culprits, now we would take a closer look at them.

Allowed to generalize, I reckoned that Fund managers were, on the whole, a pretty vain lot. It was important for them to blow their own trumpets, professionally speaking. This was probably even a necessary survival trait, since they were likely only as good as their last monthly performance. The more they were known and respected, the better their job endurance prospects. This individual would assumably be hard-wired to both accept and act on tips, since they were vital to his performance and ultimately, to his compensation. Vanity was a powerful thing. So, armed with the names of these five Funds, I set out to speak to Mike.

I asked Mike to search for any literature on any of the Funds, especially marketing collateral – brochures and such – that might show photographs of the Fund managers themselves. I wanted to see if I could ID either of the two Wolf conspirators that I had overheard at Tobacco Road. I was certain that at least one of them would prove to be a Fund manager.

Mike came back to me within three hours. He dumped a bunch of printouts on my desk and said that he would have some more the next day. I skimmed through the material and came up with a hit within five minutes. The other man talking to the Fat Guy at the restaurant turned out to be Mr. Miles Cunningham, Fund Manager of a couple of the largest Funds at the Manitoba Regent Bank, known around town as MRB, or Mister B, befitting its status as the second largest bank in Canada.

Simon found an unused whiteboard and we took a lot of pleasure in sticking Miles' picture onto it. This was now a proper investigation. We added the name of the holding company that Simon had found and below it the PEIT affected daughter companies. We also added the names of the suspect Funds, the names of their Fund managers and the bank controlling each.

By the end of that week, we had six holding companies listed on our whiteboard. Each of these had between three and five daughter companies listed below it, each of which had PEITed at some point in the last two years. Those dates were listed next to the relevant company. Mike had found photographs of some of the Fund managers and these too were posted on the board. We were making progress.

We re-read the scant file compiled by the deceased Alan Summer and could only add one company name to the whiteboard. It was unconnected to any of the holding companies and had not been involved in any PEITs of its own because it was unlisted. We wondered if this might be a company that Summer had thought was connected to Alpha. We gave it a space of its own on our board. It was called White Wall Investments Inc. White Wall was incorporated in the province of Ontario and had an address in Mississauga. A Mr. Gatleen Mani was listed as the sole director. We sicced Mike onto Mr. Mani to see what he could come up with. We also tasked Mary to investigate any trades undertaken by either White Wall or by Mani himself.

Mike discovered that Mani had once owned a couple of franchise operations in the Greater Toronto Area. He had sold out five years ago for $1.6 million and now appeared to be retired. Mary found zero trades in Mani's name but hundreds in the name of White Wall Investments Inc. It seemed that Mr. Mani had funded White Wall with the proceeds of the sale of his businesses and was playing the market through White Wall. The trouble was that he wasn't very good. Fully half of his trades were loss making. The rest were between mildly positive and flat, with one very obvious exception. This was a $52,250 bet on Toronto Switchgear, a large trade by Mr. Mani's standards. He placed the order two days before the stock rocketed from $9.50 to $19.80. He sold a day later, pocketing a cool 108 percent. Interesting.

"That's so obviously an inside trade," I said to Simon. "But it doesn't feel justified enough to make it into the Summer file. There has to be something else here."

"I reckon he knew someone, who could have been from Alpha, or even one of the Funds and that someone gave him this tip," postulated Simon. "He also trusted him enough to make it a 50k punt, which for Mani was quite a big deal."

"I'd love to talk to him," I said.

"So, lets do it then, lets get out of here!" declared Simon, getting up. "What are the OSC going to do, fire us?" Good point.

We told Mai See at the front desk to let DS Parry know that we had gone out to get some fresh air and some fresh perspectives on the case. She started demanding we do it ourselves, but Simon lifted his eyes to the 19th floor, suggesting Parry had been summoned to the executive suite. She took our message.

We rode the Rocket down to Union station, then bought a pair of tickets for the Go Train to Mississauga. It took us an hour in all from OSC headquarters to Mississauga station. When we get there, we found a taxi and Simon gave the cabbie the address for White Wall. He seemed to know where he was going. It took us another twelve minutes before he pulled up outside a medium-sized residence in a moderately affluent neighborhood.

"Is this it?" I was surprised.

"Yes, this is it," he said, waggling his head.

"Can you wait for us?" I asked him.

"Sure, sure. You pay first ride, I wait second ride," he said.

Simon paid the guy and we watched him pull up under the shade of a nearby oak and pull out his Hindi newspaper. It looked like we had secured a ride back.

We walked up to the front door and pressed the bell. A small dog started barking immediately. Amid shushing sounds, an elderly East Indian gent opened the door. "Can I assist you?" he asked formally.

"Yes, actually we are here to see Mr. Gatleen Mani," Simon said somewhat officiously. He flashed his access card. "OSC," he told him.

"I am himself," said Mr. Mani extending his hand for a shake. "How do you do?" We shook hands. His good manners left us a little flummoxed until Simon saved the day by asking him if we could come inside. "Certainly, be my guest," said Mr. Mani, but you could tell that he wasn't comfortable with the invasion. Neither was his dog.

Mr. Mani fussed about offering us tea, something to eat, even the bathroom. He eventually seated us to his satisfaction in the living room. I noticed a stunningly beautiful girl, mid-twenties, pictured on his mantelpiece. "Is that your daughter, sir?" I asked to break the ice.

"Yes, that is she," he said.

"She's beautiful," I enthused. "Stunning actually. She could be Miss India."

He developed a great big smile. He was happy that I had noticed and said, "Thank you, thank you, and quite married now, quite married." I didn't know what to say to that.

"Mr. Mani," Simon started. "We're investigating some irregular trading activities on the TSX on behalf of the OSC and we came across a trade that you made last year which we believe could help us in our inquiries." I noted that some of Parry's mannerisms had rubbed off on Simon. He'd also succeeded in thoroughly distressing poor old Mr. Mani.

"My...I...what trading?" he eventually got out.

I decided to take over the questions. "Sir, in August of last year you bought and sold 5,500 shares of Toronto Switchgear within a very short period – three days. In that three days, the share price appreciated by more than 100 percent. You can see how that would send up a flag at the OSC, right?" He looked confused and frightened.

"Can I be in trouble for this?" he wanted to know.

"Not if you tell us who told you to buy the stock," I said, as gently as I could. I really wanted him to give someone up, but he looked spooked.

"That's what Mr. Alan said too," wailed Mani. "But I am

telling him this was just lucky. I picked it, it flew, I won. Why can you not believing this?"

"This Mr. Alan," said Simon. "Would that be Alan Summer from our office?"

"Yes, yes, Summer," said Mani. "He is still there?"

"No, he died," I told Mani. "He was killed in a traffic accident last September in Quebec." Mani went white.

We left soon after that, believing that we had stirred the old man up unnecessarily and we felt a little bad about that. Luckily, the taxi was still waiting for us. We made the 4:50 p.m. Go Train back to Toronto's Union Station. It was too late for the office when we arrived, so we headed up to street level to find a pub with an outside patio. It was after all, a glorious Friday.

Dividend Clawback

We settled for a patio table at the Duke of England on King, a popular bar amongst the young financial set. It was also popular amongst those still trying to look young. We got to talking about Mani. I was convinced that he was telling the truth. He'd probably hit it lucky and the next thing, the OSC was all over his case. It must have been quite tough for the old guy. Simon wasn't so sure. We finished our beers and I called for the bill. With that, a group of guys standing nearby edged closer towards us, waiting to grab our seats when we left.

The waitress came over after a while, holding out the plastic billfold. As I looked up to grab it from her, I saw the Fat Guy. He was just walking in. We were screened by the standers, but I doubt he would have recognized me anyway. I stopped in mid-grab, looked at the waitress, shrugged and said, "Er, sorry, could we have one more?" She glared. "They were delicious," I added helplessly. The standers looked pissed. I shrugged at them, too.

"What the hell?" asked Simon.

"The Fat Guy from Tobacco Road just walked in," I told him. His head spun as he searched him out.

"That guy? Blue jacket?"

"Yup, let's watch him for a while." This coincidence was way too good to pass up.

The Fat Guy settled into a standing corner and ordered something from a passing waitress. She reappeared soon enough with a glass of white wine. He eyed the crowd, looking at us in the process, but I could see that we didn't mean a thing to him. That was a good sign.

The Fat Guy was halfway through his wine before he was joined by a woman. She was nothing special to look at, but she carried herself very well. She had poise.

"Simon, do you think you could get a picture of the two of them?" I asked. I was referring to his new phone, which had a 2.0 megapixel camera built into it. He thought about this for a bit then pulled the phone out, fiddled with it for a while, then with his thumb surreptitiously on the toggle, stood up and pretended to be having a phone conversation. I could see him aiming his camera sideways through our screen of standing guys. After a meaningless conversation, he sat down again.

We waited for a while, then he called up the media file, and we took a look at the pictures. The first two were totally useless because he had his finger over the lens. Then he must have figured it out because it moved away and we got a perfect, but slightly washed out picture of the Fat Guy. The next couple of shots only revealed glimpses of the two of them, because there was a very persistent stander between us and them who kept getting in the way. Simon would have to try again. Just then, he pointed his camera at me and took two quick pictures. He was focused on a spot to my rear at the time. I turned to see the Fat Guy and his consort walk out behind me and stand partway in the street. They hailed a taxi. Before we could even call the waitress over to pay up, they were gone. The good news though was that Simon caught the lady in a perfect profile shot.

We arrived at the office the next Monday behaving like conquering heroes. With a flourish, Simon tossed his phone pictures onto his desk and picked up the unsorted pile of Fund manager photos that Mike had left us. Sure enough, halfway through the pile, we found the picture of Mme. Maxine du Toit. She was from the Montreal Bank of Commerce and was the lead manager for its five largest Funds. None of the MBC Funds had been involved in the PEITs as far as Mary's reports were concerned, so she must have been doing it more cunningly, we reasoned. So, onto our whiteboard went her picture, right next to Miles Cunningham. "You're busted, lady," I said.

Better than this, though, was that we now had a picture of the Fat Guy. We gave it to Mike. Simon told him not to come back until he had written a name, address and place of employment on the back of it. Mike looked at him strangely.

"You know, I think you're beginning to enjoy all this," I told Simon. "Fact is, I'm quite enjoying it too. At least it's a real job. Now that we don't have a million dollars anymore, I might stick around after this gig."

"Let's not get too excited," Simon admonished. "And let's not go telling Parry just yet that we're converts to his cause. I want to keep my options open." He was right, of course. There was no margin in volunteering any information around here.

It developed into a productive few days for us. We rounded out our missing Fund manager mug shots, finding them all. We also made a pretty good stab at listing all of the executive officers and senior managers in each of our six holding companies. We had to purloin a second whiteboard. Nobody complained.

"You know, something worries me about Mme. du Toit," I admitted to Simon one afternoon. "Our trip wires are very effective, and yet none of her Funds seem to be caught up in this."

"Hmm, maybe just not yet," Simon offered. "Maybe the Fat Guy is still working on her."

That afternoon, Parry dropped in for a quick update. It seemed that today he really had been called upstairs and it presumably had something to do with our case. We showed him the progress we'd made on the board: the names and photographs of the Fund managers, the photo of the Fat Guy, and the names of the senior personnel at the target companies. Again, Parry was impressed. We then launched into our sojourn to Mississauga and our meeting with old Mr. Mani and his face darkened. He let us finish, then he let rip.

"Who authorized you to discuss this case with Mr. Mani? He demanded.

"Nobody, we did it on our own initiative," I said, proudly.

"That's right. It was not authorized. How do I know that?" he sneered, "Because I do the authorizing around here. You are NOT authorized to approach any of these people under investigation! Am I clear on this?"

"Crystal," said Simon. I nodded, peeved.

"What else?" he asked.

We told him about our recent thoughts on Maxine du Toit, that we might have seen the Fat Guy trying to recruit her. He was interested in this development. It defused his anger. I could sense him figuring out how to best use this information.

Parry checked his watch. It was 14 minutes to the hour. "I need to get upstairs," he said, and pushed off. No doubt via the street level for a smoke first.

As Parry left, Mike came in. "Got him!" he announced. It took us a while to realize that he was talking about the Fat Guy. "Meet Mr. Ainsley Pascal of 385 Brunswick Avenue, Toronto. According to his tax records, he owns Larabee Investments and passes himself off as an Investment Consultant working from home."

"Good work, Mike!" said Simon with feeling. He rotated his office chair and began scribbling this info onto the board. "Now, where exactly is this place?" He asked.

"It's in the Annex, just north of U of T. Not far from where you guys live, actually,"

"And how would you know where we live?" I wanted to know.

"Aah," said Mike, turning away and tapping his nose. He was smiling.

After he'd gone, Simon said to me, "I'm curious, aren't you? I want to see this Brunswick Avenue place; get a feel for what we're dealing with here."

"What part of NOT authorized do you not understand?" I said, a little exasperated.

"Look Eric, as far as I'm concerned, these dirt-bags have cost us our million dollars. If Parry didn't have such a hard-on for Alpha, we wouldn't be here, we wouldn't be his patsy cheap labor!" He was working himself up. "And," he continued, "I have no intention of allowing this exercise to take a minute longer than it needs to. I want it done! I want to get the hell out of here and re-start my life." Simon paced around, his impatience with the situation apparent.

"Well, sure," I started.

He wasn't done yet. "Which means, that if I think that watching something, or talking to someone, is going to make this go faster, then that is exactly what I am going to do. If Parry wants to fire me for that, then wonderful - same objective, different mechanism." I kind of expected a "Clear?" at the end of that.

It didn't come, so I said "Clear." He didn't laugh. But come to think of it, he was absolutely right. As usual.

Change of Control

We got home, ate some leftover takeout, and set off for a stroll through the Annex. It was going to stay light for quite a while at this time of year. We could see the buds starting to form on the mostly bare trees. It would soon all spring to life.

Since we lived nearby, we knew the way. It was fairly straightforward. Toronto was pretty much laid out in a mighty grid pattern. We crossed Bloor then turned into Brunswick, heading north. We walked through tightly packed, but beautifully built traditional Toronto homes. Many of these dated back to the late 1800s, with some painstakingly restored. Most were built of red brick, with some on a sandstone base. The trees lining the street were old hardwoods, a little difficult to identify without their leaves, but which would no doubt look majestic in the summer. In the midst of all this splendor was a student fraternity house. It was run down and looked out of place in this otherwise affluent suburb. The byproduct of close proximity to a university, I supposed.

After a few minutes, we walked past number 385. This one had a front garden which was in the process of an early spring makeover. The house itself was well-maintained and orderly. We couldn't see inside, but felt that it would be pretty neat and tidy. We continued our stroll for another 100 yards until we reached a convenience store. It was run by a pleasant woman with a rich East European accent. We bypassed the selection of Hungarian goods for sale in the store and bought a couple of cokes. We took them outside, where we leaned up against the bicycle stands and aimed our sun-glassed eyes on number 385.

It took an hour before we got any action. A yellow Prius taxi pulled up against the curb and 30 seconds later, Ainsley Pascal, formerly known as the "Fat Guy," waddled purposefully out of his house and eased himself into the back seat. They drove right past us. I could see Pascal consulting his Blackberry and the cabbie looking up into the rear view mirror—one giving and the other receiving directions. A step ahead of me, Simon had the good sense to punch the taxi plate number into his phone.

"You think he has no car?" asked Simon. "If not, we might be able to track his movements through taxi records."

"Let's take another look," I suggested, and we turned back and walked slowly passed Pascal's place once again. There was no parking slab in front, no city parking tax tag on display anywhere, and no undercover parking of any sort attached to or in the house. There was also no space between the house and either neighbor to allow a car through to park at the back of the house. "I guess not," I mused, "unless he's using the street."

"Fat boy like that?" said Simon, looking skeptical. "I doubt it."

We stopped in at Lexington's for a beer on the way home. It was a student dominated pub with lots of disjointed rooms and patio's, yet all interconnected and somehow promising a coherent purpose. It was pumping as usual, but the beer was cold, the non-smoking, rear facing, upstairs patio was breezy and we could talk. And think.

"Let's see what we got," Simon started counting off on his fingers. "We got PEITs. We got Pascal selling, or giving, PEITs to Fund managers. We got the names of tainted Fund managers receiving same from Pascal. We got Mr. Mani, who may or may not be complicit in this. We got the names of potential sources of inside information from the parent companies of PEIT affected companies. The one thing we do not have," Simon finished, "is any hint of who is pulling the strings."

"Could that be Pascal?" I wondered. "We're going to have to look at his financials carefully to see if he's substantial enough to be the 'big kahuna' here. I doubt it though. Something tells me that Pascal is the pawn of someone more serious."

The following day, Parry called us into his office. As this case heated up, so our interaction with DS Parry had escalated. We brought him up to speed with regards the Fat Guy's identity and told him about our stroll of discovery through the Annex. I took pains to explain that we were far away and never approached him, that we hadn't even thought about it. He glared but didn't chew us out again. We had tested a new boundary with Parry today and it seemed like we'd gotten away with pushing it a little.

"Well, I wanted to bring you two up to speed with what's going on up there," Parry said, his eyes flicking up to indicate the offices upstairs. "They're bringing an Assistant Crown Attorney into the scene now. You are to give him your full cooperation, of course."

"Of course," Simon joked back.

Parry looked unamused. "His real purpose is to assess the evidence and then to make a determination on whether or not this case remains with us at the JSIU. If he thinks that current and future evidence can stand up to even more scrutiny, then he'll recommend we prosecute under the criminal code of Canada. This means jail sentences for those involved." This time, Simon looked impressed. "Then, the case will be transferred to the Integrated Market Enforcement Team. They're with the Royal Canadian Mounted Police."

"Clear," we called out simultaneously.

Parry frowned but continued, "Yes, well, this stiffer burden of proof is all about intentions. We have to prove that inside information was *knowingly communicated* from someone intimate with the secrets of the company concerned and that it was *knowingly used* by the recipient, either for profit or for the avoidance of loss."

"We definitely have the jail term scenario with this case," Simon said quickly. "How long before the RCMP take it over?"

"Not so fast," replied Parry. "IMET can request civilian assistance and I have already placed your two names on their list. They'll probably co-opt our whole team, in which case we will all simply get a new boss. The only difference then will be that we will need to figure out how we prove the *intentions* of our various suspects."

"I'll tell you how," I said. "We need to get out there and rattle some cages, get someone to turn in Mr. Big. I seriously doubt that all of the corporate information traffickers are doing this willingly. Knowingly, perhaps, but not *willingly*." I wondered if he got *my* emphasis.

"All right, Mr. Hanson, let's see a plan of action then. We'll reconvene here tomorrow first thing."

"Clear," I said, annoyed that Parry had trapped me into coming up with a plan.

Mary called by to tell us that according to her calculations, Pascal's company, Larabee Investments, was investing no new money. It was essentially reinvested profit that was churning through different trades. Furthermore, at least 85 percent of Larabee's trading profits of some $5.2 million, had involved PEITs. It sure seemed to me that the OSC had enough to bust this guy on, but was he Alpha? Was Alpha just a $5 million business?

We went to see Mike. His news was that he could find absolutely no link between Pascal or Larabee and any third party company. He also thought that it was unlikely that Pascal was our Mr. Big.

In the end, we reached the same conclusion. Pascal was not the man. That being the case, Pascal, and possibly others like him, were doing Alpha's bidding. Pascal's real job was working for Alpha. His job was (minimally) to get the information to the Fund managers. He might also be playing a role in obtaining the information from the target companies. That last thought remained to be tested. But he was probably being remunerated for all this by being allowed to trade the PEITs, which he did privately through Larabee.

It took us the rest of the day to put some cogent bullets together that might be construed as a plan.

The next morning, as instructed, we reported to Parry first thing. He had a visitor already, who turned out to be Assistant Crown Attorney Peter Sheldrake. He looked harried. We were introduced and then Sheldrake sat down and we got on with the business of conferencing with Parry.

Simon outlined our plan. It was simple enough. We had two identified targets: Pascal and the Fund managers. As much as we would love to, we believed that bringing any of them in would compromise catching Alpha. We reasoned that Pascal and the Fund managers already had what appeared to be a solid relationship, and a mutually complicit one, so any pressure on the Fund managers would probably result in a warning to Pascal. Additionally, any pressure on Pascal would probably result in a warning to Alpha. The exception here was Maxine du Toit, who we sensed was not yet inside the Pascal circle of trust. She might be the weak link that we could squeeze.

"To what end?" ACA Sheldrake wanted to know.

"To wear a wire at her next meeting with Pascal and get his

intentions on tape," I explained, "then hopefully we can put pressure on Pascal to give up Alpha."

Parry and Sheldrake looked at each other. "That works legally," said Sheldrake. "Can you make it work operationally?"

"No," admitted Parry, "we would need to involve IMET and the RCMP."

Just then, Mary knocked on Parry's door, came in, dumped a print-out in front of me and declared, "I think we're in the middle of our latest PEIT." Sheldrake looked confused. Parry went silent and Simon and I quickly opened Mary's latest run of the PEIT Report, scanning the now familiar columns.

"She's right, look here," said Simon pointing, "Eastern Harvesting Machinery has just shot up almost 30 percent. Volume is through the roof."

"Extraordinary!" proclaimed Sheldrake, clearly impressed, but not sure why.

"EHM is 50 percent held by Eastern Consolidated," I explained to Sheldrake, "one of the holding companies suspected of providing Pascal with inside information."

"Excellent!" he said, rubbing his hands together. I'd never actually seen that done before.

I drilled deeper into Mary's data to see whether or not the five MBC Funds managed by Maxine du Toit had participated in this latest PEIT-fest. They had not. Good, our plan could still work.

Parry picked up the phone and placed a call to IMET GTA. It looked as though this case was going to get kicked upstairs.

IMET sent their man around to the JSIU offices at the OSC the very next day. Their man was Inspector Hicks. Hicks looked like a fit and trim, but aging, marine. He was square-faced with short gray hair and he looked like he would nicely compliment a pair of combat trousers. Right away we could see that this guy meant business. Even his card was straight to the point – Inspector Hicks, IMET, and a phone number. He seemed to have the resources available too.

On his first day, he called a meeting with Parry, Simon and me, Mary, Mike, Sheldrake, and two others. One was introduced as Ms. Davies from the Department of Justice. The other was introduced as a tactical expert from the RCMP, named Lai. We were in the spare office on the opposite side of our bullpen from Parry. This was to be Inspector Hicks' office.

Hicks thanked all of us, especially Detective Sergeant Parry for our contributions. He then politely dismissed Parry and Sheldrake to get on with the business of the JSIU and the Crown, respectively. Thus, as Parry and Sheldrake made their way out, power was neatly transferred to Hicks. He then asked Simon and me to bring everyone up to speed. That took about an hour with various questions from Hicks, the DoJ, and Lai. When we got to the part where we'd seen Pascal get into a taxi, Hicks made a note of the cab company and the taxi plate number. He told Lai that he would action this and would have Pascal's taxi rides followed. We finished with where we had ended the previous meeting with Parry, that being our recommendations with respect to Mme. du Toit.

Hicks didn't immediately like that idea and turned doubtfully to Lai. "Is this doable?" he asked.

"Yes," answered Lai, "we lift her, bring her here, explain her position, mike train her and send her out to wait for contact."

"DoJ?" asked Hicks

"No conflict there," replied Ms. Davies.

"Right, do it," Hicks said to Lai. Turning to address us all he said, "Meeting adjourned, thanks everybody, have a good weekend." And just like that, the kidnap, intimidation and recruitment of Maxine du Toit was set in motion. We were all business now!

Fill or Kill Order

Maxine du Toit was in the habit of taking the TTC to Rosedale,
then walking the short distance to the place she rented on
Ramsden Park Road. She didn't own a car. She would then do
the opposite journey in the morning, which is when members
of the RCMP tactical unit nabbed her. By the time we made it
into the office just before 9:00 a.m. that Monday morning,
Maxine was already sitting in a conference room on our very
18th floor. Inside with her were Ms. Davies and Inspector
Hicks. We could see them all quite clearly through the half
glass wall. They were all drinking coffee. Maxine looked as
though she had been crying and Hicks was berating her. He cut
a menacing figure.

Eventually, Ms. Davies extracted a slim stack of papers from
her briefcase and placed it in front of Maxine. She looked a
little stunned, but shakily read through each page with Ms.
Davies pointing things out and explaining things to her. It
ended with Maxine signing the document and Ms. Davies
pulling out a rubber stamp and doing to her what Parry had
done to us all those weeks ago.

Maxine then excused herself to the bathroom and stayed there
for some considerable time. When she came out, she looked a
lot better, but something had been taken out of the poise we
had first noticed.

Someone new, the Technical Guy, was waiting for her when
she returned. He handed over a silver cylinder which looked
like a lipstick holder. She played with this under his direction
for a while then they sat there talking. Eventually, she fiddled
some more, then dropped it into her handbag.

Then it was our turn. Hicks called us in and introduced us.
"Eric, Simon, Mme. du Toit has kindly agreed to assist us with
our inquiries into the insider trading case involving Mr. Pascal.

We are indebted to her for this act of civil duty. I want you gentlemen to get Mme. du Toit up to speed on the investigation."

I kicked it off this time. She insisted we call her Maxine, so we quickly got on first name terms with her. Without giving her any names, corporate or personal, I explained how we had five Fund managers dead to rights on insider trading charges and how grateful we were that Pascal was unable to get to her too. I explained theory of the PEITs and how we used this to unequivocally prove the insider trading case against Pascal. We discussed some of the technicalities of the trap we had laid so that she was similarly convinced that Pascal was guilty. Simon then explained how the OSC wished to pursue criminal charges against Pascal, rather than an administrative fine, and in order to do this we needed her to get Pascal to admit his *knowing intent* to defraud the market with this inside information.

She thought about all this, then nodded to Hicks and said, "All right, Inspector Hicks, I'm convinced. I'm ready to do my part." Then, she extracted the lipstick holder from her bag, twiddled it, and we all jumped back as it suddenly burst out with the sound of my voice explaining PEIT theory.

Hicks smiled and said, "Well it seems to work all right, my dear," like she really was one of the team and not a conscripted near-felon. We got dismissed from the meeting and the three of them continued with her training.

After she had left, Hicks dropped around to give us some addresses to work on. It seemed that the taxi company dispatcher had cooperated. He had given up some of the places that he remembered his cabbies taking the passenger from 385 Brunswick Avenue. Our job was to try to match these with the various companies and banks uncovered so far in the investigation. Grunt work, but necessary. While with us, he mentioned that Maxine had been told by Pascal to watch

Eastern Harvesting Machinery stock. She figured that this had been his way of proving his credentials to her. She would use this as a pretext to call him to set up a meeting, at which she would record the discussion. It sounded good.

Maxine turned out to be a natural. She recorded almost everything, so when she came in a few days later, she had the whole nine yards laid out for us. We listened intently around the conference table as she turned her lipstick recorder to playback. It started with a loud tapping crackle, and in the background, the line buzz of a telephone ringing on the other side of a phone call. Maxine explained that this was her calling Pascal. The crackle was from her positioning her lipstick recorder up against the handset of her office phone.

A man's voice came on, "Hello?"

Then the unmistakable sound of Maxine with her rich French Canadian accent, "*Monsieur* Pascal? This is Maxine." She was inclined to emphasize the last part of her name so that it sounded like Maxeenah.

"How are you, Maxine?" Pascal greeted her. "Did you see those EHMs take off the other day?"

"Yes, I did, and I was very impressed with your foresight, M. Pascal, how did you, ah, work this out?"

"Well, I have friends in high places, Maxine, and again, please call me Ainsley," chuckled Pascal.

"*Mais,* why of course, Ainsley. You suggested last time that we get together again, *non*? Are you free to meet soon?"

"Well, yes, I would be delighted." We could hear him shuffling papers. "Are you free tonight?

"For you Ainsley, absolutely. You are my new best friend! Where would you like to meet?" flirted Maxine.

Pascal thought for a bit then said, "What about Friar Tuck's, on Yonge? Would you meet me there at seven?"

It was as though Pascal had deliberately picked a place close to Maxine's house. How would he have known that?

"Perfect," responded Maxine without missing a beat.

Maxine explained to us that she had walked over to Friar Tuck's that night and met Pascal. They enjoyed some great food, some expensive wine, and lots of chit-chat. Then the subject of EHM and the market started to come up, so she excused herself, went to the restroom and turned on the device. Back at the table, the conversation continued.

"Ainsley, you know how difficult it is today to make money in equities? The market has corrected but the recession is not over. Now just *petit* gains are to be celebrated. But my Funds, they have to have a minimum proportion of equities, it makes me crazy."

"Yes, I know," commiserated Pascal. "Which is why moments like EHM can be so special. As I said earlier, I will send you whatever other information I get."

"What do you want from me in return?" she asked.

"Whatever tips you get. We all need all the help we can get."

"But Ainsley, I get stock tips every day. Every day! Very few of them work, and even those have never been as good as EHM, they are usually too late already! I don't think that you will find my tips interesting, not when you have quality information like EHM. Tell me Ainsley," she says stroking his ego now. "How do you come across such good information?"

"I have friends..."

"Yes, yes friends. We all have friends. But yours are special, *non*? Are they from inside the company?"

She must be really charming Pascal because he's keen to impress her, "Yes, from the company," he admits.

"Aah, you rascal!" Maxine says playfully. But you could sense that Pascal was loving it. "So you probably also do some front running before you pass it to me! Very clever Ainsley, very clever."

"Yes, it is quite clever, I agree, but hey, we all have to make some money somehow, Maxine."

From there, the conversation went general, and Maxine shrugged, switched off the lipstick device, and handed it over to Hicks.

"Thank you, Maxine," said Hicks. "You have played a very important part in this case. We appreciate your efforts." Maxine just held out her hand and stared at him. He eventually got it, cleared his throat, nodded at Ms. Davies, and then smiled sweetly as he watched Ms. Davies hand Maxine her original stamped contract. When Maxine left us, her poise was back.

"I guess that's it for Pascal?" asked Simon.

"Yes, this should get him jail time," confirmed Hicks. "More importantly, it will give us the leverage to encourage him to cough up Alpha." Hicks was extremely confident he'd get what he wanted. I guessed he had dealt with more than a few Pascals in his time.

It was therefore a massive blow to us all when Lai came in the next morning to announce that Pascal was dead.

Whistle-blower

Hicks immediately mustered us all in the conference room to give us the bad news. We were shocked. It was undeniably a murder. Pascal had been shot in the forehead, just inside his front door. The killer had only taken Pascal's laptop.

"That makes it potentially number two," remarked Lai, obviously referring to Pascal's demise.

"Number two? There was another murder?" I asked.

"Potentially," said Hicks. "We've been looking into the death of Alan Summer. We found some inconsistencies."

"What inconsistencies?" asked Simon. This hit close to home. We'd read his file, sat at his desk, and we had probably both used his office coffee mug. "Are we in danger too?"

"I don't know, probably," admitted Hicks.

"Oh, nice!" Simon said sarcastically.

"Fact is, we don't know who's behind this, so we can't be sure how much danger you're in," explained Lai. "I do know, however, that very few people were aware that we had something on Pascal, most of whom are in this room." He let that sink in. Did we have a fox in the hen house, I wondered? If so, it could only be one of us at the OSC. Or IMET. Or, for that matter, the DoJ, or even the RCMP. Suddenly, we saw the problem with these big task force networks.

"This Alpha has some powerful connections," said Lai. A major understatement.

Green Shoots

Pascal's funeral was that Saturday. Hicks was all over it with concealed cameras and mics and spies. He wanted to observe who all went, how they were connected and where they might lead him. Fair enough.

"But isn't it redundant if there really is someone rotten on the inside feeding Alpha this information?" Simon wanted to know.

"We have to try," said Hicks. He should have been a bit deflated and going through the motions mechanically, but not Hicks. He had everyone running hard, as if the dust storm of activity would somehow trump the possibility of a bent insider. He was acting like a pro.

Simon and I were assigned to attend the actual church service. Hicks would be outside. Lai and others would be at the graveside. We got there fairly early and each took a seat in the back corner, me left, Simon right. We had tried to memorize every face and name combination that Mike had come up with. Most were Fund managers, but he had also put pictures to the faces of quite a few of the corporate types associated with the suspect holding companies. Our job was close-up identification to augment the cameras already installed. We were to ID anyone that we could, after which Hicks would put a tail on them.

We carefully checked the attendees as they made their way into the church. Within ten minutes, both Simon and I recognized the Investor Relations Manager for Eastern Consolidated. It made sense that he was there. He would surely have been well positioned for inside knowledge of some of the goings on at Eastern. He seemed like a logical candidate for Pascal.

"Dark blue suit, brown hair, just entered," I whispered into the voice-activated cuff mic that Hicks had given us.

I saw Simon recoil violently and despite the seriousness of the situation, I laughed. His earpiece was obviously set too loud. I saw him fiddling with the pocket control just as the voice in my ear said "Roger, got him, who is it?" Simon clapped a hand to his ear because now the volume was too soft again. What a crap spy.

"That's Tim Chase, Investor Relations at Eastern," I whispered again.

"Roger."

Tim Chase walked up to the front of the church and stood in line to pay his respects to the dead Pascal. He eventually got to the head of the line. He leaned forward, tenderly stroked the dead man's cheek, stood looking at him for a moment, then walked right back outside.

"He's leaving!" I heard Simon say.

"Roger." Then silence for the next long while because nothing interesting happened. Suddenly, right before the priest started the serious business of committing poor Pascal's soul, a bunch of people who must have been waiting around outside came in to take their seats. Nobody we knew. Except that a heavy-set, muscular looking man in his late 30s or early 40s, and walking in the middle of the pack, was escorting a drop-dead gorgeous women into the church. He had blond, crew-cut hair and a magnificent tan. She was the utterly lovely, yet quite married, former, Miss Mani. They squeezed into the row two down from me on the opposite side of the aisle. She was a little older than her picture on the Mani mantlepiece, but she was nevertheless very agreeably visible in the aisle seat.

My cuffed hand flew towards my mouth to update the team,

then stopped. I couldn't explain it. I looked over at Simon. He was looking around, but not at what I was looking at. His view of her was probably blocked. I kept staring at this awesome creature, wondering what to do next.

Toward the end of the service, I had figured out a plan. I breathed to Simon, "Let's go," then got up and walked out.

"Anybody home?" I asked into my cuff.

Hicks came around the corner and beckoned me over. "Thanks, we got the guy," he said as Simon joined us. "He was just making sure that Pascal was actually dead!" Hicks thought that this was quite funny. He explained that Tim Chase had been trapped by Pascal with a Russian hooker two years ago. There were pictures and all sorts. At that time, Chase had been married into the family that owned a good deal of Eastern Consolidated. He was on a roll, but any whiff of his indiscretion would have finished him. The stress of living with both Pascal's demands and the pressure of the job soon gave way to stress in their marriage. They had separated two months ago. Divorce proceedings had begun. Chase had no doubt that he would be nudged out anyway after the divorce, but he had been hanging onto his job in these tough economic circumstances. It was mainly this which kept him a slave to Pascal's demands. That is, until Pascal died. Now he was free, he thought, so he had come down to the funeral just to make sure. He'd even pinched Pascal's cheek to double-check he was dead.

"He was a happy man when we took him into the de-briefing van," Hicks informed us. "He's telling us everything he knows about Pascal. Unfortunately, he doesn't seem to have anything at all on Alpha. He thought that Pascal was Mr. Big, which in his eyes, he probably was." We stood around a bit chatting, then I excused us and dragged Simon away.

"What was that about a party we had to go to?" asked Simon. I filled him in on the Miss Mani development. He whistled and asked, "Why didn't you call it in?" I told him that at first I didn't know but then I figured it must have been a subconscious fear that the dirty insider might get wind of it. I reckoned it was safer to keep it to ourselves, maybe try to follow them and learn something about them. He bought into this thinking.

We set off to find a taxi. There were lots of them circling the church, so we picked one and jumped in. We got the cabbie to continue circling until the people came out. He thought we were waiting to pick up another of our friends, which was a fine assumption by us.

About ten minutes later, people emerged and sure enough, there was Crew Cut with Miss Mani on his arm. They lingered a few minutes chatting to the priest, then headed for the street. A black BMW 745i immediately pulled away from the curb upstream of them and glided forward to pick them up. We wondered how long it had been there. Did the driver see us talking to Hicks? This was a bit of a worry. Despite this, Simon still managed to key the license plate number into his phone.

We asked the cabbie to follow the black car, but without being caught. We flashed him our OSC access cards and convinced him that we were with the police. Our covert chase worked well until we got onto a section of Bayview going north that was carrying no other traffic except the Beemer and us. I got the cabbie to go past, then pull over near a string of shops. Simon and I quickly opened the doors to make it seem as if we had arrived at our destination. We sat in the taxi with the doors open for a minute until the Beemer drove past us. After a decent wait we took off again after Miss Mani and Crew Cut, but this time well behind them. We hoped it had worked.

From Bayview, the Beemer turned right into Bridal Path, easily one of Toronto's most affluent suburbs. There was sufficient third party traffic to screen us so we followed them in. They turned into High Point Road. The properties were huge. Most were adorned with modern mansions built well back from the road and amidst fantastic gardens. We saw the Beemer turn into its destination. We were still well back, so by the time we reached their driveway, our targets were safely inside. We only caught a quick glimpse of the house as the massive wooden gates closed the gap between the twelve foot high surrounding walls. We got the house number though. What a place.

~~~

PART THREE : DEAD CAT BOUNCE

CHAPTERS

Golden Handcuffs
Barriers to Exit
Chinese Wall
White Knight
Ankle Biter
Chameleon Option
Black Swan

Golden Handcuffs

I tried to get all this straight in my head. Mr. Mani was an unsophisticated investor, prone to losses. Crew Cut married his daughter and either as a show of goodwill or as part of the marriage deal, gave Mani a strong tip. Mani acted on this tip and triggered an investigation by the OSC's Alan Summer. Summer approached Mani. Mani panicked and called his new son-in-law. Summer died. We got swept up in this mess. We identified Pascal, linked him to the Funds and wire tapped him using Maxine. Pascal admitted to insider trading on tape, and was then murdered. This, and Summer's death, suggested an internal JSIU leak. Crew Cut attended the funeral. If Crew Cut was not Alpha himself, then he was connected. How did we learn more about this guy if there was a snitch in our own ranks? That seemed to be the central question and between Simon and me; we didn't have a clue how we were going to deal with it.

Meanwhile, I had developed a strong crush on the former Miss Mani. I could quite see how she could be dominated and bullied by the thuggish Crew Cut. I convinced myself that she needed saving and that we needed to smash this Alpha group in order to liberate her. At least I had endowed myself with a noble motivation now.

After talking it over with Simon, we decided that the best course of action would be to speak to Hicks. Of them all, we seriously doubted that he was bent. So Simon called him and he answered immediately, even though it was Saturday evening. Simon explained that when we were in the taxi, a couple came out of the church and we recognized her to be the former Miss Mani. We'd missed spotting her in the church. We had then followed them to Bridal Path and we now wanted to give him our report on this, could we meet? Hicks picked us up 45 minutes later and we headed off to the Distillery District for a beer and a chat.

After briefing Hicks on our trip out to Bridal Path, we explained our logic that Crew Cut was somehow linked to Alpha, or could even be Alpha. Given our concerns of a leak (leading to at least one if not two deaths so far), we had wanted to keep this information strictly between the three of us.

Hicks was sympathetic and he promised secrecy. We could see however, that he was torn. It was obviously vital that we somehow learn more about Crew Cut in order to move the investigation forward. Yet his keeping quiet about it completely compromised that situation. How could he even get Mike and Mary to do some digging without a decent target in mind? Hicks pondered this situation for about half a beer, then suddenly he told us that he might have a workable idea.

"How would you two feel about some undercover detective work on Crew Cut?" asked Hicks. "This way I can get some more dope on Crew Cut without alerting them through our potential internal leak." It sounded all very plausible. Only nobody was talking about the danger.

"If you mean watching and recording, stuff like that, then I guess we could do it," Simon ventured. "What do you say, Eric?"

Actually, the prospect of watching over the delicious former Miss Mani was very appealing. I agreed. Hicks then outlined his plan.

On Monday morning, Hicks assembled the team and informed everyone that Simon and I had done virtually all that we could on this case and he was standing us down. He thanked us and said that if they needed us some more, they knew where to find us, which was supposed to be funny. He told Mary and Mike to continue to piece together the case book for the Crown Attorney. That was going to be painful work which we were pleased to be out of. We happily turned in our access cards to Mai See on the way out.

As planned, we hung around in the Eaton Center downstairs for half an hour before we were called by Hicks. We met him at the Starbucks. He gave us each a SIM card and instructed us to exchange it for the card in our phones. This would keep communications reasonably secure. He also gave us a small digital camera. It was incredibly powerful. Finally, he handed over a sheet of paper that he had just printed off. It contained the ownership details of the black Beemer. "Right," he said, "go find out who we are dealing with here and let me know ASAP."

According to Hicks' printout, the black BMW was registered to Eagle Investments Inc. That was a start. Simon got Sherlock booted and he started browsing company registers. It was amazing what you could find with a little effort. Eagle Investments was owned by one Egon Luga of High Point Road, Toronto. Well hello there, Mr. Big.

Then we turned our attention to the house. The registered owners were Egon and Jasleen Luga. Aah, Jasleen, what a great name, I thought. Hold tight, I'm coming to get you out of there.

The joint ownership was pretty normal in Canada. However, there was nothing else to be found on the Lugas. That was odd.

We left a message for Hicks that we had discovered something. He called back within the hour and we told him about the Lugas and Eagle Investments. Despite the lack of information, he sounded pleased.

Simon and I gave a lot of thought as to how we might surreptitiously put eyes on the house. It was more difficult than it sounded because we had been out there and had seen how open it was along the road. We couldn't realistically hang around on the street, or even sit in a car. We pulled up the google maps satellite image of the area, identified the Luga house, and sat looking at it for a long while, trying to figure a plan.

I could make out a fairly large swimming pool at the back of the property. It seemed to have its own pool house too. Could we pass off as pool cleaners?

"They've got a massive wall around their property. How about we try peddling our skills as painters," I suggested.

"Good idea," said Simon reflectively. "Let's give that a go."

The next morning, we went shopping. We ended up at Lowe's on Castlefield, where we sourced pretty much everything we needed to look like painters. That afternoon we busted out the new brushes and used them to dab the new white overalls with various shades of acrylic. We sloshed paint over our shoes, our caps and even our arms, faces and hands. Step aside Braveheart, we looked pretty fierce. When the paint had all dried later that afternoon we scrubbed it partly off ourselves and then took our clothes to the laundromat. After a hot wash cycle and a long tumble drying, these clothes looked as broken-in-painter-chic as they were ever going to be. We did, too. It was time to pay the Lugas a visit.

We got our taxi to drop us off at the top of High Point Road. From there, we walked towards the target house, stopping every now and then to gesticulate towards some random house or other, pretending to assess its poor state of repair. We eventually got to the Lugas. We did our inspection in case anyone was watching us, then pressed the intercom button. A male voice answered. It sounded Eastern European. "Yes?" A simple enough question.

"May we speak to the owners, please," I asked. "We're painters. Your external wall could do with a fresh coat of paint. We'll give you a free quote." This begat silence for about two minutes. Finally, the same voice burst out of the intercom, "Fine, come inside." This was accompanied by a clicking buzz and the pedestrian gate swung aside a few inches. We pushed right on in.

"Wait there, please!" cried out Egon Luga before we could even lay eyes on him. He was calling from the undercover part of the circular driveway near the front door. We waited near the gate as he made his way down the cobbled drive towards us. I found this kind of strange, that the great man himself would be doing this menial greeting stuff, but I put it down to his Europeaness. I figured that it must be a cultural thing.

"What's your rate?" demanded Luga.

"For this height wall? $20 per linear foot," I responded. I had no idea if this was good or bad.

"$15 and you have a deal," countered Luga. He probably didn't know either.

I looked at Simon. "$17.50," he said, gruffly.

"OK, deal," agreed Luga, "when can you start?"

"Tomorrow," I said. "I see your inside wall is almost worse than the outside. Do you want us to do that, too?"

Luga looked up at the wall, "OK," he said, "when you get here tomorrow, just start on the outside. When you finish that then call me on the intercom." Then he turned and went back to the house. We let ourselves out.

"Jeez, he didn't even talk about the color," said Simon, "I

would have thought that he would consult his wife about that."
He was right. It just went to prove my theory that this was a
guy who bullied his way through everything. I'd have bet good
money that the former Miss Mani would give anything to get
out of this relationship. Out of this luxury jail.

Not knowing what else to do, we flaked a piece of paint off the
wall and took it down to the paint store on Eglinton. The paint
guy did some magic with his matching system and came up
with a recipe. "You want a sample?" he asked.

"Nah, just give us ten gallons," said Simon nonchalantly.

We bought rollers, extensions, scrapers, polyfiller, and all
manner of painting paraphernalia. The paint guy graciously let
us store it all there overnight.

We made the collection the next morning in a taxi, stuffing
everything into the trunk, and after an uneventful ride we
arrived at the Lugas' house.

Simon started painting from the south side and I started from
the north. Our plan was to make our way towards the gate,
which was roughly in the middle of the wall. This way we
hoped that we could keep a constant eye on the gate, which
was realistically all we could see from the outside anyway.

The paint job looked great. So it was no surprise when at the
end of the outside project, we were invited to continue inside.
This gave us an opportunity to look the place over. We worked
outwards from the gate this time.

At midday on the third day I had reached the corner and was
collecting my painting kit together when I saw Jasleen step
through the back patio doors on her way to the pool. She was
wearing a flimsy sarong over a striking white bikini. She
looked amazing. At the edge of the pool, she stepped out of the

sarong and dived into the pool with a soft plop. She swam a few lengths very fast then leaned up against the deep end edge with her elbows out of the pool, catching her breath. I had slowed my gathering and was staring at her, mouth open, as she pulled herself out in one fluid movement to stand dripping on the edge of the pool. Her white bikini had turned slightly transparent and her nipples were distorting the fabric. I could feel myself becoming aroused. She looked at me, smiled, and then Egon from behind me said, "What the hell are you gawking at, punk?"

I spun around, shocked, spilling paint. Egon was standing four feet away, pushing Simon in front of him. Simon had his hands secured behind him and Egon was pointing a silenced pistol at the both of us.

Barriers to Exit

Egon got me turned around with my hands behind me. He
pulled a large zip-tie out of his pocket and ripped my wrists
together. Jasleen walked slowly up to me, silent, water trickling
down between her breasts, which were still heaving gently
from the swim. She stood in front of me and slowly squeezed
the pool water out of her hair, this action pushing her boobs out
suggestively. Then she dropped her hair and slapped me across
the face with everything she had. I staggered sideways, my face
stinging with shame and pain. Egon laughed.

"Take them away!" she hissed.

Egon pushed us towards the triple garage. The furthest bay had
a built-in inspection pit with steps leading into it. Egon pushed
us down there. We found a door at the end of the pit made from
steel mesh.

"Open it," said Egon. Simon shouldered it open and we found
ourselves in an underground tool cage, nine feet wide and
twelve feet long. It was completely empty. The door clanged
shut behind us and we heard a bolt sliding home. An overhead
light came on then we heard Egon's footsteps receding across
the floor above us.

"Holy shit!" whispered Simon with feeling. We were terrified.

They kept us locked underground for the rest of the day. As it
grew dark we heard a vehicle drive in and then motors closing
the garage doors. Then Egon Luga walked down the stairs and
opened our cage. "Out," he said, walking into the cage and
herding us back up the stairs with his silenced pistol doing the
talking.

The black BMW was parked in the first bay and in the middle
bay, a dark colored Crown Victoria. At the front of the Crown

Vic stood Jasleen Luga with arms folded and looking angry.
Beside her, without any expression at all, stood Inspector
Hicks.

Simon recovered first and called out to him in a croak. This
galvanized Jasleen into action and she stepped around the
Crown Vic and slapped Simon hard. "Shut up, you fucking
bastard!" she spat. I sucked in a sharp breath, not sure if it was
the violence or the language that had appalled me. I was
becoming rapidly turned off by Jasleen Luga.

She turned to Hicks and asked him, "Are these them?" He
nodded. "Fine, get rid of them!" she ordered Luga, spinning on
her high heels and walking noisily away.

Hicks raised his eyebrows at Luga. "Tomorrow," said Luga,
reading his query. Then to us he said, "Back in the hole,"
giving us a shove in the direction of the pit.

The steel mesh gate was bolted behind us once more and we
heard the garage door open above us, letting Hicks out. After a
while the garage door closed again and it went silent once
more.

Panic was setting in now. What the hell were we going to do?
The Lugas had plans to kill us in the morning, so if we had not
managed to get out by then, we were toast.

I sat down heavily against the wall and felt a sharp pain in my
right shoulder. I had felt my muscles cramping up steadily
throughout the afternoon. Having our hands cuffed behind us
was restricting blood flow. The pain was constant now, but
what I had just felt was something else entirely. I looked
behind me and saw a broken steel nail barely poking out of the
concrete wall. It had clearly snapped off, which made it too
difficult to remove with the rest of the fittings. Instead,
someone had tried to pound it into the wall with a hammer. It

had almost worked, but now the merest piece of steel nail protruded, which had a flattened head from repeated hammer blows. That flattened head had razor sharp edges.

I called Simon over and he helped me position my bound wrists against the nail. Then he directed my sawing actions. Once I got a feel for it, I cut through the plastic tie surprisingly easily. I felt immense relief when I could finally move my arms in front of me. When the feeling returned to my fingers, I grabbed Simon's wrists and rubbed his binding over the nail until it cut through. It felt incredibly good to have won this small battle.

We lay down on our backs for a while, letting our bodies recover from the stress of Lugas' constraints. After a while, we inspected the steel mesh door. It was a heavy gauge mesh welded to a steel frame. The frame was mounted into the concrete wall with enormous hinges. We were not going to break out that way.

The locking mechanism was a simple deadbolt. It was not possible to reach it from the inside, because the mesh was too small and the bolt was positioned too far over. I experimented with the plastic ties, sticking them through the mesh at an angle to see if they would reach the L-shaped bolt. They did. OK, now for our next trick. We made a noose out of one of the zip ties by feeding it's tail through itself again and leaving a loop. I used this to snag the short part of the L and lift it to the horizontal. I then used the other zip-tie, folded in half for stiffness, to push the bolt so that it opened along it's track and came free of the latch.

We were out! We closed and bolted the cage door behind us to pass casual inspection and crept away up the stairway. When my eyes were level with the floor, I carefully looked around the garage. The last thing we needed was to trigger a motion detector or wake a sleeping driver. It seemed clear, but we went painfully slowly up the stairs all the same.

The wall furthest from the inspection pit led into the house. The closest wall was the exterior wall of the garage. In this wall, close to the garage door, was a regular door. We assumed it led out into the garden. It's key was in the door. We carefully made our way over and unlocked it. It was sticky and made a loud click. I opened the door and light spilled into the garden. We slipped out, quickly closing the door behind us.

"Go!" I urged Simon. He ran as quietly as he could to our newly painted wall and then along it to the corner furthest from the gate. I followed. We got to the corner and Simon boosted me up so that I could just grab the top. Adrenalin pulled me over and I fell in a heap on the other side. Simon managed to use the inside corner to scramble up like a cat burglar. As he came over the top I saw him looking back in the direction of the house. He looked worried.

"Quick, let's go," he urged. I took it that we'd been rumbled and sprinted down the road with Simon right behind me. We made a mile before we saw a vehicle coming up behind us and we dived into the shallow ditch running parallel to the road. The vehicle cruised past. It was an orange and green painted taxi, not the Beemer, thankfully. We continued our run. The taxi was 500 yards away when its brake lights suddenly lit up and it turned to the left and up a driveway. We ran a little faster. We caught the taxi as it was making its turn back onto the road. The cabbie wasn't going to stop, but then he saw that we were painters and had probably been working late into the night. He felt some empathy with our situation. He chatted amiably as he took us all the way home. It took us about that long to catch our breath, pacify our hearts, and stop shaking.

Chinese Wall

Running up to our apartment, we decided that either Hicks or the Lugas would look for us here first, so we packed a few things into a backpack each and hustled upstairs. It was close to 11 p.m. when we banged on the door of the Chinese girls. Joy and Kelsey came to the door together wearing nightgowns. They looked worried, but relieved when they saw it was us.

"We need a favor," I said. "There are bad people looking for us. Can you hide us here?" It was an audacious question and I knew it, but options were few and far between for Simon and I just then.

The girls looked petrified now. Eva came out to join them and they huddled for a quick conference in Cantonese. Eva was shaking her head, she said something and the others seemed to agree. They came over to us and Kelsey said to me, "We know somebody that can help but you must give them money."

"That's fine," said Simon. Kelsey nodded, turned to Eva, and said something to her, and then she and Joy raced off to their rooms. Eva stood with us and we explained to her that a bad policeman and his civilian friends were trying to kill us because we knew a secret about them. We described the Lugas and Hicks and asked her to make sure that all of the girls said nothing to them. Just then, Joy and Kelsey appeared in jeans and hoodies. After a bit more conversation in Cantonese between them, Eva pulled out her phone and started looking up a number. She held the door open for us with one hand and worked the phone with the other.

"We go," said Kelsey, and led us out the door.

Eva's phone had set my mind racing. Virtually all phones had built in GPS units these days and it made perfect sense to me that ours were reporting our position to Hicks through his fancy

SIM card. After all, we had used similar technology to alert us to tripwire events in a previous life. I mentioned this to Simon on the way down the stairs.

"Good thinking, Eric," he acknowledged.

When we got out of the apartment block an east-west College streetcar was just slowing at the stop to let someone out. Kelsey and Joy were steering us south down Spadina.

"Give me your phone," I demand of Simon. I took both of them and as I walked past the open streetcar door, I slid them in across the floor where they came to rest under a bench. The street car was virtually empty at this time of night. I doubted that anyone saw me. That should throw Hicks off the trail for a while. Hopefully someone would pick the phones up and carry them even further off our scent.

Right across the street from our apartment was the ATM that we always used to draw cash. Simon had the Housekeeping Fund card. He drew out the entire $680. Then he withdrew his maximum from his personal account and I did the same. We had nearly $1,500 between us.

Kelsey and Joy then led us to a convenience store on Spadina, right in the heart of Chinatown. The sign said it was open. It was one of those places where I doubted the sign ever said 'closed'. We went in to find a small woman dressed in drab Chinese working clothes standing on a box behind the counter. She recognized Kelsey and Joy immediately and broke into a lengthy conversation in Cantonese.

"This Mrs. Lee. She want $800 for one week," said Joy.

"That's okay, Joy," I said. "What about food?"

After another fairly long conversation between the three of

them, Kelsey said, "You buy here." I marveled at how all that got reduced to one line in English. Then there was silence and all eyes turned to us. I was a bit confused.

"I think she wants the cash, Eric," suggested Simon. I counted out $800 and Mrs. Lee snatched the money away and stuffed it into a pocket. She quickly took us to the door in the far corner of the store that was marked "Staff Only" with something below it in handwritten Chinese. The door led to a washroom straight ahead and stairs going up to the right, doubling back on themselves. We barely had time to thank the girls for their help before Mrs. Lee hustled us up the stairs to the second level. Off the landing was another door, which she opened onto a small bedroom. This contained only a bunk bed against the side wall and a little window looking out over the street. She said something in Cantonese and disappeared. Then she came back and repeated the same message, only louder and more insistent. This time she beckoned us, palm down, to follow. She took us down the passage and showed us the bathroom. The floor and walls were tiled. A western toilet sat regally in the middle of the cramped space and a hand shower hung off a short pipe immediately above it. Various plastic containers were stacked in the corner. This was going to be interesting.

Our room was noisy. The clamor of people, traffic, and street cars outside competed with the racket from the store directly below us. We could hear Mrs. Lee speaking to her customers, the bell over the door ringing them in and out and a television that we had noticed hanging on the wall opposite the counter. It was tuned very loudly to a Chinese station.

"Well, at least this is a lot safer than home," said Simon.

True. Distressing, but true.

White Knight

Our new digs kept us awake for long stretches so we used the time to come up with a plan. We weren't sure who to trust. We had been horribly wrong with Hicks. How about Parry? He had invited IMET in to the case, but was he in control of who IMET sent in? Maybe Parry called Hicks directly.

"Wait. We're missing something. If Parry is dirty, why go to all the trouble to recruit us in the first place?" asked Simon. He'd boiled the issue down again. Yes, there was no reason we could think of to distrust Parry. So, now we needed to think of a way to contact Parry without giving ourselves up to any of the Alpha-Hicks conspirators. I had the makings of a plan for that.

"Let's get to a computer," I said. We went downstairs. We bought a hat and pair of sunglasses each from Mrs. Lee and with our new disguise walked in search of an internet cafe. The Hyun Muc Coffee Shop & Internet Cafe was 40 yards away on the same side of the street. We bought Vietnamese coffees served in thick china cups and settled in behind one of Sherlock's distant ancestors.

We tried Facebook. No Parry. Same story for MySpace. We eventually found him on LinkedIn. In order to connect with him, we needed him to confirm us as a contact. We set up a profile in the name of Peit Alpha, hoping that this would get his attention. The system allowed us to personalize our invitation to Parry to join our network. We sent him a message that said "Hicks is dirty. Can we meet? D&S." The reply address was a Hotmail account we had set up just for that purpose.

We used the downtime to get some food. I found a take-out joint down the road that sold me two large clam-shells of BBQ pork with rice. We ate these at the internet cafe, checking the Hotmail account periodically. Suddenly, we saw an email pop up titled "re : Join my network on LinkedIn." This was Parry! His response was short. "SW cnr Dundas/Spadina 16h00 today. Drive by pick up BHFK going south." He had given us the plate letters of the car that would pick us up at 4 p.m. outside our LCBO. This was only five minutes away, so we returned to our digs above the store to rest up and think some more.

I had somehow dozed off despite the cacophony downstairs when suddenly Simon jumped down from the top bunk and shook me awake. "Eric! We got trouble!"

I heard sirens then. Looking out the window, I could see three cruisers converge on a spot a few shops up the street from us. A dark blue Crown Vic was already parked at an angle, half on the sidewalk, just in front of the Hyun Muc Coffee Shop & Internet Cafe. Shit, these guys had some powerful cyberware. A moment later, Hicks appeared, frog-marching the poor Vietnamese boy-manager out to his car and slamming him face down against the hood. Double shit! I looked at my watch and it showed 3:15 p.m. Time to get the hell out of here. "Let's go!" I said to Simon. It felt as though we'd been saying that a lot lately.

We got downstairs and turned right towards the staff toilet. There was a window above the commode wide enough to push our backpacks through. We followed, landing in a pile in the alleyway between Mrs. Lee's shop and the block where Hicks and his cruisers were stationed. We both cut ourselves getting out. We turned right and ran down the alley, away from the action on the street. The alley took us to the next street over. We crossed that too and found ourselves outside an Irish pub. We went in and found a table far enough from the door that we couldn't be seen from outside, but from where we could watch the street. We had to buy a beer to stay there, but it tasted good.

We figured that Hicks had somehow monitored Parry's email. Our LinkedIn message must have forwarded an alert to Parry's regular email address. Had Hicks been monitoring Parry's email, he would have seen this. We supposed that Hicks would have broken into Parry's LinkedIn account and seen our message exchange. Then he must have traced the messages back to one of Hyun Muc's computer IP addresses. He certainly appeared to have good technical resources at his disposal.

Although we had a technical explanation, we still worried that Parry might be tipping off Hicks. We knew that we had to approach our meeting with Parry carefully.

We flagged a green and orange taxi down right outside the pub door. I explained to the driver that we were looking for a friend and wanted him to drive south down Spadina, cross Dundas, then find a way to keep circling past the LCBO on the corner. The cabbie took us down Spadina, straight past the scene of the recent police action. Only one cruiser was still outside the internet cafe. Then as we approached Dundas, I saw Hicks sitting in his Crown Vic 200 yards short of the corner. He was watching the pick-up location carefully. We continued past the LCBO and saw cruisers on either side of Spadina, covering both directions. The cabbie drove past the cruisers and turned right onto Queen Street West, the only place he could do that. His next right turn was onto Bathurst going north. Finally, he turned onto Dundas going east to complete the rectangle. We got back to the LCBO about ten minutes later. We reasoned that if Parry came by at 16h00 as planned and failed to pick us up, he would probably circle around and try one more time.

The cabbie was on his second circuit when I stopped him halfway along the Queen Street leg. I explained that we would walk back and wait for our friend. The cabbie took the fare and drove off. Simon and I stepped into a Queen Street camping store and waited. At 4 p.m. we moved into the doorway. We wasted a long time getting our backpacks sorted out, all the while watching the intersection of Queen and Spadina. At about four minutes past four we saw Parry's blue-gray Crown

Vic nosing its way into Queen Street. We let it approach, watching the corner for either a following cruiser or Hicks. Neither appeared. They had seen him waiting in traffic, looking around for us, not connecting and eventually having to move on. They guessed he would go around.

At the last minute we stepped into the street right in front of Parry. He was a good driver, stopping smoothly. We jumped into the car ducking down in the spacious rear seat area and getting our backpacks into the front.

"Go around again!" I cried. "This time we'll point out a few interesting landmarks!"

We got him to go around in a wider circle so that we could drive south on Spadina, towards Hicks. We pointed out the lone cruiser outside the internet cafe, then lay down and brought his attention to Hicks in his Crown Vic and the two cruisers further down the road. Parry then did some evasive driving, looking constantly in his rear view mirror. He got onto the Gardiner Expressway cleanly and headed east out of town. We pulled into a roadside bar in the Beaches area. Its biggest asset was a parking area under some trees around the back where we could hide the Crown Vic from the road.

We got settled in the bar and Parry asked, "Do you two want to tell me what's going on?" We did. All of it.

Ankle Biter

We were sitting in a corner booth at the window which faced the rear car park and Lake Ontario. The back wall was behind Parry. Separating our row of booths from the parallel row further in, away from the windows, was a service aisle. An emergency exit was built into the back wall, accessible from the aisle. I was staring idly at this exit and sipping my beer. Simon sat back, concluding our briefing. Parry took a long drink from his glass.

The emergency exit suddenly opened and Luga came in fast, followed by Hicks. Luga had his silenced pistol out and he sat down next to Parry and jammed it hard into his ribs. Parry winced. So did I, because at that moment, Hicks poked his gun into my side. Luga leaned over and grabbed Parry's 9mm from the holster under his left armpit.

"We're tracking your car, stupid!" Hicks said nastily to Parry. He pulled three sets of police handcuffs from his inside jacket pocket and put them on the table. "Put these on," he ordered. I hesitated for a few seconds and Hicks elbowed me hard in the face. Blood poured out of my nose. "Now!" he said menacingly.

When we had all cuffed ourselves, Hicks put $20 on the table and stood up. He pointed his gun quite openly and so did Luga. Nobody appeared to take any notice of us. We were corralled out of the emergency exit and straight into Luga's Beemer. Hicks sat in the front covering the three of us crammed into the back seat. The only consolation was that I was bleeding all over Luga's calf-leather seats.

"Nice escape the other day, boys," said Luga. He definitely had an accent. "This time we aren't taking any chances. We'll just kill you straight away." He laughed and accelerated out of the parking lot.

We headed north east through Scarborough. There seemed to be plenty of places around here where three dead bodies might turn up and not cause much of a stir. Luga and Hicks seemed to have a plan though. Luga's phone went off after ten minutes of driving. He answered in a foreign language. It didn't sound like anything I had heard before. He looked at us in his rear-view mirror as he talked. Then he laughed again, much harder and longer than before. He was clearly talking about us, probably to his psychopathic wife.

I had given up. Parry sat in the middle, separating Simon and me. From what I saw of Simon, he had given up, too. His shoulders were slumped. He looked beaten. I sat back in my seat and rubbed my nose with cuffed hands. Tears were welling in my eyes as Luga finished his conversation.

I felt Parry nudge me with his left foot. Reassurance? He had one leg either side of the drive shaft. He nudged me again. It was creepy, so I gave him a dirty look. I saw that he was looking down at his left foot. I looked down there too and saw that he was wearing an ankle holster. In it, I could just make out a gun.

I was sitting directly behind Hicks, so I supposed Parry wanted me to use the screen of the seat-back between Hicks and I to get his gun out. I started coughing and blood started flowing again. I leaned forward in pain and deftly unclipped Parry's ankle holster. With the next coughing fit, I lifted the gun out and held it trembling in both hands where Hicks couldn't see it. It was a snub-nosed revolver of some sort. The safety catch was above the trigger. I moved it off without alerting Hicks.

I wondered if I had to load it. I made the motion of cocking this pistol by moving one hand over the other. Parry caught this in his peripheral vision and moved his head side to side as if in defeat. At the same time he motioned a hammer cocking action with his thumb. I got it immediately. I felt the hammer with my thumb and while looking directly into the face of Hicks, pulled the hammer back and shot Hicks three times through the seat-back. The little Kel-Tec P32 mousegun jumped in my hand as I fired it, which was just as well because it placed the second bullet a little higher than the first. It went into his heart. The third .32 caliber nickel jacketed bullet caught Hicks in the throat, by which time I think he was already dead. One of the bullets passed straight through Hicks and on through the windshield.

Luga slammed on the brakes, yelling and grabbing for his pistol while the big Beemer stood on its nose, the ABS brakes howling. He managed to get a shot off at me. I felt hot air exploding out of the barrel of the silencer and heard the bullet strike the window just left of my face. The glass starred rapidly and then disintegrated. Parry hooked his handcuffed hands over Luga's head and pulled back hard with the metal connecting chain against his throat.

"Get his gun!" Parry bellowed.

I dropped Parry's gun and went for Luga's instead. I held it pointing safely away but Luga just kept pulling the trigger as Parry slowly throttled the life out of him. He ended up putting eight holes in the Beemer's roof before he died.

"Handbrake," grunted Parry. It was between the seats. I pulled it and the big car came to a skidding stop in the gravel off the side of the road. We sat there breathing hard with rush hour traffic streaming past us.

Chameleon Option

Eventually, Parry suggested I look in Hicks' pocket for the handcuff key. I extracted it and Parry got us all unlocked. We first dropped the back seat-backs forward then inclined the front seat-backs. This way we could haul Hicks and Luga directly into the trunk without showing them off to the passing traffic. Parry got into the drivers seat and started looking around. "Aah," he said picking up a remote control fob. "Dollars to donuts this gets us into the Luga compound," he smiled starting up the Beemer.

He told us on the way over to Bridal Path that we had to move fast before Mrs. Luga had a chance to act. We didn't know if she was the end of the Alpha line or not. If we didn't isolate her quickly, we might never get another shot at Alpha. I was all for it. I had a score to settle with this bitch and so did Simon.

Parry's need for quick action had another effect too. It forestalled the shock of killing Hicks and Luga. Our self-imposed urgency was now dominating our thoughts, which worked to suppress the terror we'd just escaped. Parry further occupied our minds with questions on the layout of the Luga compound; distances, angles and features.

By the time we turned into High Point Road it was getting dark. We had the BMW high-intensity headlamps discharging brightly for maximum glare. The freshly painted Luga wall shone back at us magnificently. Parry turned into the driveway and depressed both buttons on the fob. We saw the big gate opening. As it grew wider we could see that the right-hand side garage door had begun to lift too. Parry drove quickly into the garage and hit the buttons again. The door started to close. He killed the engine and got out, standing to the side of the door leading inside. Parry had retrieved his big 9mm, I had his mousegun and Simon had Hicks' 9mm. We crept into the house quietly.

At the sound of the door closing behind us we heard Jasleen Luga calling out, "Egon?"

Parry tried to fool her with a simultaneous coughing "Yeah". She immediately shot him a question in that strange language we had heard in the car. She had been walking closer but now stopped. We didn't answer. Then we heard her running away from us. We just failed the password was my guess.

Parry took off after her. It seemed as though she was trying to get upstairs in a hurry. Parry shouted out, "Stop!" But the footsteps continued, faster. I got past Parry and sprinted up the stairs. I saw Jasleen turn into a room and slam the door closed behind her. Parry, Simon and I arrived at the door at about the same time. Parry tried to force it open. It was very solid wood and would not budge. He pushed us to the side and, taking aim at the door lock, he pulled his trigger three times. The blasts in the passage echoed off the walls and thumped into our ears. I couldn't hear what he said next. He was shouting through the door. Then he slammed against it again and it flew open. Simon and I stumbled in after him.

He was still shouting as Jasleen lifted her arm and aimed at him with a mean-looking pitch-black Glock. Parry fired. His 9mm jumped in his hand. Jasleen took it square in the chest and looked confused for a while before she hit the floor, knees first. Simon walked up to her while she was on her knees, snatched her Glock away with his left hand, and slapped her face hard with his right. She pitched over into a fetal position on the deep pile carpet.

Parry ran forward and spun her onto her back, "Who else is in on this?" he demanded. She smiled groggily, her expression said that she wasn't telling us anything. Parry put his fist on her bullet wound and pushed, hard. She screamed with the pain. "Who?" he yelled, increasing the pressure.

"Fuck you!" She spat, just as blood flooded her mouth. I could see the life leave her eyes. Parry pounded her chest in defeat. He eventually got up. We looked around the place. It was an office. IMET would probably find a mountain of damning evidence here and recover a bundle of ill-gotten gains, but it felt like a hollow victory with no-one left to arrest.

Black Swan

It was three days later when Parry called around at the apartment. He'd brought a six pack of Canadian Lager with him.

"You two did a great job," he informed us happily. "I'm here to officially offer you full time employment with the OSC, assigned to the JSIU and working for me.

"Forget it," said Simon.

"Yeah, Detective Parry, shove it," I told him. Although this came out politely, I meant it sincerely. Delayed shock had begun to set in and Simon and I were working hard to deal with it.

Parry informed us that Luga was Albanian. The chances were pretty strong that the Albanian mafia were working alongside him. He wasn't sure whether or not we'd knocked out Alpha, but the OSC had the software and strategy now to pick up any similar activity quickly. He said he would let us know how this case progressed but we doubted we would ever see him again.

We finished the beer and told Parry that we were going to work on raising the finances for Saskwatch Airways. He liked the idea and promised to be one of our first passengers. Yeah, right.

Then suddenly, he had to go. He stopped at the door, "Oh, I nearly forgot," he said producing four envelopes from his inside jacket pocket. "These are your final paychecks." He gave us each two and then took his leave.

One envelope held our regular OSC slave wage. The other pair contained checks in our respective names, drawn on our broker for $583,750.00 each, in consideration for the liquidation of our BCIC portfolio. Talk about a surprise happy ending!

Simon convinced me that this was appropriate compensation for all that we had suffered through. I didn't take much convincing. That kind of money sure did make up for a lot.

We worked out that our Punto Lanzas had only been sold once the shares had hit $56. I wondered what our OSC PEIT tripwires had made of that!

~~~

PART FOUR : CAPITAL FLIGHT

CHAPTERS

Accreditation
Incorporation
Start-up
Customer Acquisition
Competitions Law
System Crash
Kickback
Rapid Expansion
Cash Cow
Mission Critical
Decision Gateway
Corporate Ethics

Accreditation

"Turn right to heading 090 degrees," commanded Jeff, my flight instructor.

Complying, I brought the Cessna 172 out of its straight-and-level flight northwest over Lake Ontario and made a smooth turn to the right, keeping the bank angle below ten degrees. VFR flight is 90 percent about visual reference points, so I should be looking outside most of the time. I spot-watched the compass move through 135 degrees and checked my altimeter as I straightened out. I had lost about 40 feet and corrected this instinctively with backward pressure on the yolk. I glanced guiltily at Jeff. Yes, he'd seen it too.

"All right, take us home."

I had the conversation with Air Traffic Control down at Toronto Island's City Center Airport and got clearance to land on the 3,000 foot runway 06. This brought us in over the lakeshore and featured the Toronto skyline ahead of and to the left of us. The pilot's seat of the Cessna was a brilliant afternoon vantage point, with the sun setting behind us reflecting off all those acres of glass. It was almost a crime to have to get busy with my approach maneuvers. I set the flaps and reduced airspeed to start the descent. The runway looked surprisingly narrow this far out, but I was always grateful to experience its wide embrace on late finals. Today I came in too fast and ended up floating for a while before we settled onto the tarmac. I throttled down and let the Cessna roll to taxi speed with a light brake application, then I headed back to the Beaver Flying School hanger.

"Right," said Jeff as he walked around from his side of the aircraft. "You've got room for improvement, because everybody does, and don't you forget that. But your airmanship skills and your control touch have improved to the point where

I can let you go solo. We'll start that phase tomorrow, okay?"

I was ecstatic, especially since I knew that I'd not been at my best today.

Simon landed about 30 minutes later. He was already flying solo and was a natural born pilot. I waited for him to finish his post-flight briefing and gather his stuff together. Then we headed over to the parking lot where two brand-new Harley Davidson CVO "Fat Bob" motorcycles sat waiting for us. Mine was painted Opal Blue and Simon's Cryptic Black, both with the Hellfire Flames on the gas tank and loaded with every possible factory option. Man, they looked sweet!

We jumped on the bikes, started up and roared across the wide parking lot to the ferry. The Billy Bishop Terminal Building lot was connected to the mainland by a ferry that ran every 15 minutes over the Western Channel, a stretch of water only a few hundred feet wide. Bikers got a backhanded priority because they could position us on the pointy end of the ferry deck, presumably where regular cars couldn't fit. This meant we got off first. It also meant that on a sunny day, the ferry was a nice place to sit on your bike with the lake breezes in your face.

So this was our life at the moment. We didn't do anything else; just the training for our private pilot's licenses. We got to the BFS hanger every day and did some ground school and some flying. The ferrymen got to know us well. They usually came over to say hello, and I suspect, to admire the bikes.

We docked on the far side and as soon as we were able to get going again, headed back into town and to our apartment. We had decided to keep the old apartment on Spadina and College. It made no sense to change. We planned to move away from Toronto anyway after we qualified as pilots.

So far we had remained surprisingly frugal. The only things we'd spent real money on were the Harleys and our flight training. After the euphoria of discovering that our investment funds had not, in fact, been confiscated by the OSC, we resisted every urge to splurge and forced ourselves to save the money.

The bikes were an important stress-release purchase. We could not forget that we had contributed to the death of a potentially senior and connected mafia member. With the least provocation, our imaginations would run riot at how many ways the Albanians could kill us, how painful this might be, and how long it might take. We needed a distraction. We also needed to know that we were trying to enjoy life because it might come to an abrupt end soon.

After 18 minutes of weaving through the Toronto traffic, we arrived at home. We had arranged with the Chinese boys downstairs to park undercover on their unused front deck, away from and off the street. This cost us a few beers and a joyride every now and then.

The next day, we did the 18 minute journey in reverse, pulling up next to the BFS hangar. Jeff was already there and the nervous excitement was building in me.

"You know what you're doing, Eric," Jeff advised after I had gone through the pre-flight checks with him. "Enjoy yourself and just remember what I always tell you – don't get behind the aircraft."

This was Jeff's way of telling me to fly pro-actively, anticipate how the aircraft would behave and what inputs it needed from me to make it happen smoothly. Too many pilots had come to grief because they fell into the trap of reacting too late, sometimes catastrophically, to unanticipated situations that could quickly compound a small error into a cumulative disaster.

My first solo flight was fantastic. I could recall Simon telling me a week earlier how great he had felt after his first solo. I had blown it off at the time, but I certainly understood it now. I started feeling like a pilot, not a student. It was wonderfully liberating. It also gave me the confidence to do more. In no time at all I was flying solo cross country.

We passed the knowledge test and soon enough we passed the practical flight test, too. It was a proud day when we finally received our PPL documents. We had promised ourselves that when this day came, we would celebrate by flying to Prince Edward Island together. As it turned out, we settled for a celebratory day of cross-country flying to Collingwood and back. That was the first time that just the two of us flew together. It renewed our commitment to Saskwatch Airways.

The day after we got back from Collingwood we started our night endorsement, float endorsement and VFR OTT rating simultaneously. We got these in record time, flying most days and some nights.

We planned to get into the field of commercial flight. As such, we needed commercial pilots' licenses. This involved more ground school, a lot more instruction, and a whole lot more flying. We could see how young people would find this career path frustrating. It's expensive to fly the larger aircraft and you require 200 hours before you can apply for the CPL. This requires that you get a job that puts you in the pilot's seat, but for which you're not yet fully qualified. There aren't many of those jobs going. Simon and I however, were much luckier. We had money and we had time. So for convenience, we remained with the Beaver Flying School and together with them, devised a hectic schedule to train us in the shortest possible time.

Our final challenge was the instrument rating, which took

another month of intensive study and flying. By the end of this process, we were very competent pilots.

Because we had to fly so much to qualify, we undertook flights to all parts of Eastern Canada. We used the time to explore the north, the lakes and even some of the east coast. We occasionally took the girls with us. Kelsey and Joy loved it. Eva wasn't so sure. This was probably the most expensive research ever conducted, but in the end, we found what we were looking for.

It was a desolate mining camp in the Quebec wilderness called Cross Lake Copper, a newly restarted joint venture, owned by Wolf Copper Resources and the Chinese Government.

Incorporation

Simon and I clinked wine glasses with our old boss. We hadn't been back to the Tobacco Road since we'd left all those months ago, but it hadn't changed much. It was still the noisy, busy cash cow it had always been and was still as difficult to get a table. Fortunately, we had connections.

"We promised to be back to spend some money here," I said to the boss.

"Any money is always welcome, guys," answered the boss.

He looked relaxed now, but earlier he was shocked to learn about our escapades since the last time we had spoken. The boss had always been prone to swearing and even blasphemy, but this lunch had tested that inclination to new levels. Every new piece of our story was punctuated by an ever more incredulous "Shit!" from the boss.

"So where to from here?" asked the boss.

"Well," said Simon, "we've been playing with the idea of going into business."

"Not in the restaurant trade, surely?" blurted out the boss, clearly concerned.

"No, the air services business." I told him.

Simon elaborated our plan for getting licensed, then buying a floatplane and starting a small charter company together.

"When will you get your licenses?" the boss wanted to know.

On cue, we pulled out our shiny new fully endorsed "Commercial Pilot's Licenses – Airplane" and handed them over.

"Shit, would you look at that!" he beamed.

Canada was the kind of wild country that needed this service. The trouble was that it was full of one-man airlines and the competition was fierce. Our best bet was to establish a new route early, we told him. We believed that we had the opportunity to do just that with the discovery of the copper mining JV out in the Quebec boondocks.

"What the hell are you waiting for?" demanded the boss.

"Money." said Simon. "Eric and I have a million between us and we need to raise about $500k to make it all work."

"You're friendly with the money boys," I explained. "They eat here all the time. Could you give us an introduction or two? The only guys we know with money are either dead or in jail."

The boss chuckled, then said, "Leave it to me, boys, I'll need to think about this a bit and talk to someone. Today's Friday. Why don't we get together at my house for a BBQ this Sunday and I'll have some information for you then, okay?"

"Sounds great, boss, thanks!" I said.

"Just one more thing, lads," said the boss, "call me Ken. My wife's name is Tina and I actually have a dog called Boss!"

He wasn't kidding. Boss was a Rhodesian Ridgeback who met us with both front paws on top of the four foot high gate in front of Ken's house. His tail had a mean swish. We left the bikes outside and walked in, glad that our leathers protected against the pawing and licking. Ken came out and whistled once. Boss immediately turned and trotted over to sit by the front door.

"They were bred to hunt lions, you know," Ken told us. I could easily believe it. Boss was big, with a smooth brown coat, slightly raised in an elongated whorl along the ridge of his back. When he got excited, this ridge was raised making him look bigger still. "These dogs are fearless," explained Ken. "I've seen one hold its ground against a charging lion. The dog lured the attack away from its master so he could shoot the lion at a decent angle."

"Before it got the dog?" Simon asked, concerned.

"Yeah, seconds before!" confirmed Ken. "Come inside and meet Tina." With that, he led us into their hallway. I noticed a few pieces of African art blended in with their contemporary style.

Tina was a delight. She was short, immaculately dressed, and effortlessly charming. She loved to garden, which was evident in the fantastic back yard.

We sat in rattan chairs arranged around a glass table on a covered deck built into the garden. The roof was ivy over glass and it was open to the elements on three sides. One of the corner supports was a brick chimney and below this, facing into the enclosure, was Ken's built-in stainless steel BBQ.

"The beers are in here," Ken said opening a refrigerator under the counter. "Next round you help yourselves."

We talked and ate and drank and generally had a great time. Ken cooked us some lamb chops, some stiff maize meal porridge that he called *sadza* and a spicy tomato and onion sauce to go with it. Tina produced a knock-out salad. As he was opening the second bottle of Chilean *Reserva*, Ken said to us, "Now, I promised to speak to someone about your venture, and I did. I spoke to Tina yesterday." We were surprised, but interested.

Ken continued, "I've been thinking of semi-retiring for a while now and selling half the business. But what's stopped me is that I didn't know what I wanted to do with either the money or the time. That is, until Tina and I had a chat yesterday about the two of you and your plans for the future." He paused there, took a sip of his wine and continued, "I want to make you lads a proposition. I'll give you $500,000 for 36 percent of the company. I'll be an active partner. I'll manage the ground side of things and you guys do the flying. I think you know that I can manage people and money, but you'll also find that my experience with getting stuff done in countries with very little infrastructure could help this effort, too. What do you say?"

I looked at Simon. He was smiling. He said, "I'd welcome it, but why 36 percent?"

"Hopefully, the three of us will agree every business decision beforehand," answered Ken. "At the very least, in a three-way partnership, things are going to be run by majority rule. Two of us are always going to have sixty-something percent versus the other guy's thirty-something. But if we all pull in different directions, then I would like the deciding vote. My 36 percent against either of your 32 percents. Make sense to you?"

"Sure, I get it," I said. "Let me talk it over with Simon." We got up and walked into the garden. Ken and Tina busied themselves clearing up. It took us about 30 seconds to accept Ken's proposal. It was more than fair and we could definitely do with his help. The private equity boys downtown might have angel financed us, but probably for at least 60 percent of our company. I doubt they would have managed our back room, either.

"Welcome aboard, Skipper," Simon joked when we returned. We all shook hands happily.

Start-up

We named the company Bald Eagle Air Transportation Inc. Its sole asset at start-up was a 1956 De Havilland Otter DHC-3/1000 amphibious floatplane, capable of landing on either land or water. We found it in Winnipeg, Manitoba. It was a solid white converted air ambulance that was being used by the local parachute club and they sold it to us for $1.2 million. The internal configuration was convertible, from ten seats which folded down from the fuselage and rear bulkhead, to a completely open stretcher area/cargo space, or some hybrid configuration in between.

The original Otter came with a 600HP engine. This one had been upgraded to the 1000 hp PZL ASz-62 power plant driving a four bladed prop. This was a short take-off and landing (STOL) workhorse and it was perfect for our purposes.

We spent a couple of weeks up in Winnipeg familiarizing ourselves with the aircraft and doing the conversion, then we flew it back to Toronto.

Meanwhile, Kelsey had designed a line drawing of a bald eagle in flight above the words BEAT Inc that became our logo. We had this painted onto the tail in burnt orange. We added a livery stripe on either side in the same color to break up the white and our Otter was ready to fly.

Ken had been active, too. We had needed a base that was inexpensive, close to both our intended market and some major infrastructure, and accommodation-friendly. He found us something on the outskirts of Ottawa.

On the bank of the Ottawa River sits the Ottawa/Rockcliffe Airport, which is attached to the Ottawa/Rockcliffe Water Aerodrome. The two are integrated by means of an aircraft-friendly ramp which extends the land-based system into the water. Not far from there, Ken had found a bit of farmland along the river for rent. We would be able to use the attached building as a staging area for the business and accommodations for ourselves. With time, we would probably look at putting a ramp and jetty in the water.

Our prospect, Cross Lake Copper, was 218 miles north of Ottawa. From high altitude, the geological striations were clearly visible running across the Canadian Shield from southwest to northeast. These striations were usually weathered a little deeper than the surrounding rocks, so melt-water from the icy winters gathered in them to form thousands of lakes, many of which remained oriented the same way. Secondary striations ran from southeast to northwest, and every now and again, they intersected. The main mining camp was on the shores of an X-shaped lake, formed millions of years ago at the convergence of two such striations. The lake was logically enough named *Lac Croix*, or Cross Lake. The SW-NE leg of the cross was about 1,600 yards long. The SE-NW leg was half as long, but still takeoff and landing-friendly for the STOL-capable Otter.

There was some isolated farming and industry within a hundred mile radius of Cross Lake, none of which was reachable by road from there. The main Trans-Canada Highway ran 60 miles to the west of Cross Lake. The north-south border between Northern Ontario and Quebec was another 80 miles west of the Trans-Canada Highway. Our objective was to sell our services to the isolated Cross Lake Copper and then use that as a springboard to generate business from other mines, forestry units, farming nodes and First Nations outposts further afield.

We needed to assess our possibilities in this regard before we committed to the lease that Ken was holding. Our plan was to fly up there and chat to the miners themselves. We also wanted to check the state of the lake.

Ken decided to stay behind in Ottawa the next morning as Simon and I prepared to fly to Cross Lake. Ken dropped us off at the airport and we retrieved the Otter. We fueled up with avgas at the local Esso apron station and did a walk-around. Simon signed the credit card bill and I started up the Otter.

I checked that Simon and I were good to go, then got onto the radio, "Good morning, Tower, this is Eagle Oscar Golf One Zero, bound VFR for Cross Lake with two up requesting permission to proceed to the runway."

"Oscar Golf One Zero this is the Tower, you may proceed to runway 09 and hold short, good morning," answered an air-traffic controller from his newly-constructed tower.

I answered back, "Roger, Tower, Oscar Golf One Zero clear to proceed to runway 09 and hold short." I opened the throttle a bit and started my taxi to the western end of runway 09. I got to the hold point and waited.

"Oscar Golf One Zero you are cleared for takeoff on runway 09," said the traffic controller.

And we were off. "Roger Tower, Oscar Golf One Zero, clear for takeoff," I confirmed, turned left onto the runway, and gunned the motor. I sat on the brakes until the needle hit 1,500 r.p.m., then released and the Otter shot smartly forward. The big 1,000 h.p. engine ran up to takeoff revs of 2,200 r.p.m., I rotated smoothly, and we were airborne within 450 yards. Climb speed was 1,000 feet per minute as we turned out left over the Duck Islands in the Ottawa River below us.

The Otter had a flight ceiling of 17,900 feet, but we stayed at 5,000 feet on our heading of 360 degrees. We cruised at 125 knots with no wind. The journey at this 144 m.p.h. ground speed took us just over an hour and a half. Our navigation was spot-on, with Cross Lake appearing over the horizon like lopsided telescopic cross-hairs on a broken hunting rifle.

We circled over the lake and the camp, partly to check out the water and partly to alert them to our arrival. Then we made our approach from the southwest and touched down halfway along the southwestern leg of the cross. The mining camp was built on the central triangular patch of ground between the NW and NE arms of the cross. This area had been cleared northwards for 100 yards. At the northern edge of the clearing was a drilling machine belching diesel smoke. On the west of the clearing, near the water was an administrative hut and on the east of the clearing, also near the water, was the accommodation block. It had all clearly been helicoptered in fairly recently. The helipad was in the center of the triangle formed by the two buildings and the drilling rig.

There was no jetty to tie up to, so as we taxied up to the water's edge, Simon got out onto the float and made ready to jump for the bank. The plane edged in to within three feet of the shore before the bottom of the floats started rubbing the pebble bed. Simon jumped and tied us up to a stump. I joined him as soon as I could.

"Good morning," I called to the man leaning half out of the administrative hut.

He didn't reply. We walked closer and found two men standing around a central table in the middle of the hut. They had coffee on, but didn't make any offers. "Yes?" asked the taller of the two. He was not friendly.

"Actually, we would like to speak to the boss about air services," Simon started. "We were wondering if you could use someone like us to ferry in equipment and supplies and take personnel backwards and forwards."

"No." said the tall guy.

We were a bit stumped. There was no logical come-back for
this. We just stared. The other guy saw our discomfort and
added, "We have the chopper," by way of an explanation.

"Isn't that quite expensive?" I asked.

"No." The tall guy responded, curtly.

This was getting ridiculous. It was time to try another tack.
"Hey listen," I said, "how about a cup of coffee and we'll be on
our way?"

The tall guy looked at me for a while, then nodded to his
colleague. The other guy fished around for a pair of paper cups
and poured us each half a cup from the pot.

"We didn't introduce ourselves," I said. "I'm Eric and this is my
partner, Simon." We both stuck our hands out for a shake.
They just looked. Eventually we had to drop our hands, feeling
slighted.

"Friendly folk, aren't you?" said Simon, edgily, his body
language turning confrontational.

The tall guy said something to his colleague in French. My
French is not so good but I understood him to ask "What did he
say?" The other guy shrugged.

Aha, so that's the problem here, I thought. Some people still
thought the damn Anglo-French war was still on. I immediately
launched into my high-school-level French, trying to explain
why we were there. At the end of this, they were both cringing
at my crap grammar and even worse pronunciation. But it did
the trick – it broke the ice. They started talking now in a
mixture of English and French, less inhibited about what was

clearly to them, an embarrassing English deficiency. Once he warmed up, Simon was surprisingly good at French, which helped tremendously.

Our second attempt at introducing ourselves yielded the name of the taller guy, Michel. He was both the camp geologist and base captain. There were only seven men at the base, these being Michel and six drillers working around the clock in twelve hour shifts.

We learned that they had a company deal with a heavy lifting chopper service. This had been adequate so far because it brought in and took out good quantities at a time. Their exploration effort was still in phase one.

If the first few exploration holes looked promising, then the company planned to bring in more exploration teams and more equipment. Their advice to us was that we should come back in a few months and check things out then. If we liked, suggested the shorter guy, we could bring them some cigarettes because that was one thing they were always running short of. I figured that this lack of nicotine probably soured the mood around here from time to time too.

It was tough to just walk away now, having pinned our hopes on getting in with this company on the ground floor. I was furiously trying to think up some additional points to keep the conversation going, but my limited French was seriously constraining the process.

Suddenly, there was a loud bang from the direction of the drill rig. Both of them looked up sharply, suggesting to us that this was no normal noise. The abnormality was immediately confirmed by some excited chatter on the 2-way radio. Both of them rushed out.

We followed to see what the commotion was all about and

found them gathered around one of the drill riggers, who was lying on the ground and clearly in a world of trouble. Michel knelt down and felt the injured man's leg. The rigger screamed in pain. Then I saw that the injured man's leg was broken below the knee. There was a major kink in it. More chatter on the radio preceded a couple more men emerging from the accommodation hut. One looked as if he had just been woken up. He was carrying a first aid kit. He was told to get a move on, prompting him into a run toward his stricken colleague.

The medic found a syringe pre-filled with something, twisted off the needle cover and jammed it into the injured guy's buttock, straight through his pants. Then he ran to the admin hut and returned with a pair of splints and a large roll of duct tape. They waited until the pain had deadened a bit, then the medic pulled a roll of crepe bandage from the first aid kit and put this into the injured man's mouth. "Bite it!" said the medic.

Michel sat down and held the injured guy below his armpits and around his chest from behind. The medic positioned the splints and made ready with the duct tape. The other guy from the admin hut looked at the injured guy, nodded once then grabbed his broken leg, pulling it straight with a sickening click. The screaming erupted as everyone held the injured guy down while the medic taped the splints securely either side of his broken leg. When he was done the coworkers rushed to pacify the poor injured guy who lay in the dirt, spent, whimpering and still with the coiled bandage in his mouth. Somebody kindly removed it.

I looked over at Simon and saw that he had turned pale. I hoped he wouldn't pass out.

As the painkiller took effect, Michel turned to us and asked if we could take his guy to hospital. We said, sure thing, we'd take him to Ottawa and we'd have our ground crew transfer him to a waiting ambulance. It sounded good, anyway.

The medic made a stretcher, using lengths of wood and more duct tape. Between us, we lifted the injured guy into the waiting Otter and strapped him in. It was his lucky day. Who knows how long he might have waited for a casualty evacuation had we not been there.

I got Michel's satellite phone number, and gave him Ken's cell number in return, as the BEAT office. I arranged to update him once we had the injured driller taken care of. Then Michel radioed one of his team to grab the sample boxes and, before we knew it, we had a stack of six boxes of geological core samples being lashed in place next to the supine injured guy.

These were wooden boxes six feet long, two feet wide and a few inches deep, which were internally separated into three inch wide channels. The channels held the diamond drilled cores, essentially miniature columns of rock extracted by the drill rig. The rock cores themselves were marked with depths and other stratigraphic hieroglyphics. Michel explained that someone from the company would call to arrange to pick these samples up and take them away to be assayed. Each box of samples weighed about 150 lbs. So from nothing, we suddenly had our first payload of 1,100 lbs. I think this was Michel's way of paying us back for helping out with their casualty.

Takeoff was surprisingly quick, despite the load. We made enthusiastic comments about the Otter's performance as Simon trimmed her for a straight and level cruise home at 5,000 feet.

Thirty minutes out of Ottawa, we picked up cellphone signal and called Ken. We explained our position and asked him to arrange with the airport to have an ambulance standing by. Ottawa/Rockcliffe is a relatively small airport, so this incoming emergency caused some excitement amongst the various departments. This had the ATC checking with us frequently and cleared us straight in to runway 27. They even had the airport fire engine out halfway down the runway. I don't suppose it got out much. Anyway, they deserved full marks for covering all the bases.

After successfully transferring the injured guy to the ambulance and unloading the cores into Ken's truck, I called Michel, the geologist to give him an update.

"Thank you Eric, I will put in a good word for your Bald Eagle." he promised.

We all felt pretty pleased with ourselves as Ken drove us back to our temporary motel.

Customer Acquisition

The next morning, we drove over to the Realtor's office and signed the lease agreement. It was for a two year initial term, month-to-month thereafter. This was fine. If the business took off, then we could re-negotiate or move somewhere better. The great thing was that the landlord was prepared to give us occupation that very day, as soon as the checks had cleared.

Our efforts over the next few days focused on getting the place set up. Ken went back to Toronto to fetch Tina, Boss and our bikes.

The homestead was huge. It had eight bedrooms, which had obviously been planned for the holiday escapades of a large extended family. One of the rooms was a kids' dormitory. The house had two living rooms and a giant kitchen/dining area combination looking out over the river. The front living room had an attached open patio accessible through glass sliding doors. Outside were well-developed shade trees, but the garden was run down. There was also a separate two car garage.

Ken's organizational skills were quickly apparent. He arranged it such that the garage became the warehouse and the front living room became the office. The sliding doors became the office entrance. I printed out one of Kelsey's designs, cut it into a stencil, and spray-painted our logo onto the door glass. It looked great. We commissioned a local sign writer to make us signs for the driveway and the garage doors.

Tina took charge of the office administration, the garden, and the house. Boss never left her side.

BEAT Inc. received its first phone call the following day. Wolf called Ken to arrange collection of the samples. They were headed to a laboratory in the Cryvilla Industrial Park, less than four miles away as the crow flies. Ken immediately offered to transport them there in his truck. If anyone knew how to build customer loyalty, it was Ken.

We got off to a flying start with Wolf. They commissioned us to perform a weekly service. Each Tuesday we would receive a fax with the names of personnel to be transported up to Cross Lake and the names of those to be relieved and returned to Ottawa. It was usually four in and four out and took place on Thursdays.

In the build-up to flight day, we received boxes of supplies, dropped off by various vendors and stored in our warehouse. This was mainly consumables, but also some equipment. Empty sample boxes also needed to be returned with the outbound re-supply run. We also started a personal account for each member of the exploration team. They would hand us a list of stuff they needed each week and we would bring it out to them.

Our return leg relief run carried the four relieved team members, the geological samples and any equipment that needed repair.

Tina got four of the better bedrooms straightened out. She offered these to Wolf to house their relief team in the days leading up to their flight back into the wilderness. Soon fully occupied, these rooms became the exploration team's home away from home.

Ken built storage lockers for each of the exploration team. They kept their personal stuff in here which allowed for the rooms to be freely rotated. It also gave them a good reason to continue to use our services. Tina cooked meals for the guys too, which was probably the real secret behind keeping the occupancy rate at 100 percent. We were starting to generate multiple sources of revenue for Bald Eagle Air Transportation Inc. Now we needed to widen our client base.

Simon and I took this issue up and started cold calling the owners of the mines, camps and farms in our operational area. This was the most frustrating part of the exercise. Invariably we had to leave voice mails. On the strange occasion that we got to actually speak to the right person, we would be told to send him or her an emailed proposal, which we always did. But as compelling a case as we believed we were making, we were met thereafter with absolute silence. Numerous follow-up calls were attempted, but we never got to speak to that person again. A mental picture began to emerge, of all these corporate types spending their day dodging ringing telephones, avoiding voice mails, and ignoring emails. This evasive activity had to consume a huge amount of corporate resources. Wasn't it a lot easier, I wondered, for them simply to do their jobs?

"What do these people do with their day?" I asked Simon in frustration. "This is driving me insane!"

Finally we'd had enough and decided to bypass the bureaucracy. We selected our top three business prospects and planned to fly straight in and introduce ourselves. Our prospects were a logging camp, a mining operation, and a farming village. We learned what we could about them and took off late the next day.

First stop was the logging camp. We touched down on the adjoining lake and made our way over to the main activity center. It was late afternoon, planned this way because we needed an excuse to stay the night. We had brought an almost full load of meat and beer, both delicacies in a logistics-challenged environment.

We walked up to a knot of men standing around a freshly prepared fire. They looked like they had recently dunked in the lake after a hard day's work.

"Afternoon," said Simon. "Who could we talk to about sharing your camp for the night?"

"Yes, I am Alain, in charge of zem," said one of older men in a thick French accent. We introduced ourselves in our terrible French. Alain-in-charge turned out to be a nice guy and offered us food, too. "We have no beer though," he admitted.

"We're taking some beer and food to a mining camp further north," I told him, "I'm sure that they wouldn't mind if we shared this with you and replaced it later." There were excited shouts and very soon we had 20 hungry, thirsty takers. We unloaded a box of prime sirloin steaks and four cases of beer. The steak went onto a grill over the fire and the beer went into the lake to chill. It was a fine BBQ.

Once we became friends, I asked Alain how they got re-supplied. It turned out that the loggers never got relieved. It was a seasonal job, so the gang of them came in and left *en masse*. Twice weekly supplies were brought in by Quebec Air floatplane, which from the description was a Cessna 206. This aircraft had less than half the payload capabilities of the Otter, which probably explained why luxuries weren't possible. I told Alain that we could bring him more stuff weekly than the current operator was doing twice a week. This had to be a major saving since the flying costs were similar enough. Plus, didn't they deserve a beer or two after a long day? We gave out our new business cards.

The next morning, Alain came to wish us goodbye. "I will have a word with our head office about your company," he told us.

"Good luck with that," remarked Simon dryly. "When was the last time you actually spoke to someone there?"

Alain laughed, "Yes, voice mail, always voice mail! Maybe I will leave a message that we have changed our re-supply carrier. They do not like to call back my sat-phone," he said half jokingly, "Too expensive!"

We wondered about that on the way to our next destination.

This time, we landed on the grass strip belonging to the farming village of Randville. We didn't expect much. These were hardy farming folk who lived very remotely with very little use for anyone from the outside. There was, however, a collection of buildings arranged around an open square about 500 yards south of the runway. One of these buildings was a pharmacy and probably our best prospect, so we went inside. We met the pharmacist who explained that everything came into the village by road. The only need for emergency arose medically from time to time. When this happened, they would usually take the victim by road to the nearest hospital at Amos 70 miles away. This took two hours. If the victim needed further help, then that hospital would arrange the evacuation.

We told the pharmacist that our plane was actually an air ambulance and that we had experience with casualty evacuation. We left him our cards in case. That afternoon, we left for the mining camp to repeat the events of the previous night.

North Gouin Exploration was further advanced than Cross Lake. It had eight exploration rigs working and a total staff of 27 people. They had a professional camp manager named Claude running the show. He seemed to know exactly what he was doing. NGE was situated on the north shore of the Gouin Reservoir, a large lake system 250 miles NNE of Ottawa.

The stay-and-party ruse worked just fine this time, too. We said that the beer and meat was left over from our last stop. Because this was a much more established camp, they grew some of their own vegetables, so this BBQ had sweet potatoes to offer as well.

According to Claude, they were re-supplied by Quebec Air three times a week. Sometimes an extra flight was necessary for equipment, for which he had to plead with Quebec Air to make available. NGE had eight guys rotating in and out weekly, split into the three flights. It was a scheduling headache for him. We pitched the benefits of BEAT Inc. again – higher payload, higher passenger load, translating into a cheaper, more regular schedule twice a week. We also weaved Tina's hospitality component into our proposal. He loved it.

It was Claude's responsibility to arrange all logistics. He didn't need to refer this decision to anyone, so he hired us on the spot. He looked as though he truly relished the prospect of firing the arrogant Quebec Air on their next supply trip. Then, he showed us his plans for developing a grass strip close to the camp so that he could keep the camp running all year round. "Get skis for your aircraft," he instructed.

Competitions Law

Naivety prevented us from worrying about any sort of reaction from Quebec Air. We had just aggressively pitched two of their customers, stealing one of them. A big one.

Tina fielded the phone call. After listening for a while she covered the mouthpiece and said, "Ken, there's a very rude man on the line. Do you want to take it?"

"Yes?" inquired Ken into his phone.

"I want to meet with you clowns," came the voice.

"And who might we clowns expect to meet with?"

"Felix Gerard, Quebec Air. I take it you're the guys responsible for stealing my customers and disrupting the market?"

"Are we responsible for your crap service too?" Ken could be caustic too.

"What?"

"Never mind. Let's meet for lunch at the Wingman at Ottawa/Rockcliffe tomorrow."

"That's in Ottawa, pal. I'm in Quebec," said Gerard testily.

"So I hear, pal," Ken rejoined. "I also hear that you've got a plane. We'll see you tomorrow." He hung up on him.

It just so happened that Simon and I were back from re-supplying North Gouin Exploration and were available for lunch. We biked over to the Wingman which was a stand-alone building on the edge of the O/R apron. It was so convenient to flyers that the owner had joked for a long time about creating a drive-through for aircraft. The food was usually good, too.

When we arrived, we found two strangers talking to Ken in one of the booths. They were leaning forward over the table and into his personal space. The older of the two, a man with faded red hair and a bloodshot face, was making a point aggressively. Ken looked calmly back at them both. We walked up and I slid in next to Ken. Simon dragged a chair over and placed it at the head of the table, effectively sealing the booth off from escape. That changed the social dynamics a lot.

Ken introduced us. The redhead was Felix Gerard and his sidekick was called Martin. "These gentlemen were just complaining about our predatory business practices," said Ken smoothly, looking at Felix as if inviting him to continue. No-one said anything for a while. The waitress took this as a signal to come over and take our orders. We all ordered hamburgers. The Quebec Air contingent ordered theirs to go.

Martin started it up again after she left. "Listen, Mr. Gerard is only concerned that as newcomers to this market, you might upset the commercial landscape," he insinuated, "perhaps without even realizing this." He had the claustrophobic seat, hemmed in between the booth divider behind him, the table in front of him and the exterior wall to his left. He shuffled about in his corner trying to get comfortable both physically and mentally.

"In what way exactly?" asked Simon. It was obvious that he wanted Martin to spell it out and incriminate himself.

"Well, you see," Martin began, flustered. "Quebec Air is ideally placed to service certain customers. We are ideal for all the remote locations in an arc 45 degrees either side of Quebec City and up to 350 nautical miles out. This means practically an area from Quebec City to Amos and then circling around to Port Cartier at the mouth of the St Laurence." He drew this imaginary area on the table in front of him. Gaining confidence he continued, "We are in Quebec, serving Quebec province to our north. You are in Ottawa, Ontario. We were wondering why you don't turn your attention west to your own province? If you did this, you could serve the whole area from the border region near Quebec, northwest to Sudbury, south past Georgian Bay to London and east again through Toronto to Kingston. Ottawa is ideally positioned to service that region." Again he drew the area for us.

"Lots of fishing trips to the Algonquin too," chimed in Gerard, stabbing a point on the table in amongst Martin's table maps. I noticed that he seemed happy to let Martin do most of the actual collusion to allocate markets. I wondered which of them would tackle the price fixing component. It didn't take long to find out.

Mistaking our silence for acquiescence, Martin soldiered on, "We also noticed that you have priced your service very aggressively," he stated. "There are not so many of us operating in Quebec that we need to take this stance. It's destructive for all concerned. We end up simply destroying value and only the customer wins, without themselves having done anything for it. You are at least 20 percent below the market price. That pricing level would be more acceptable to us if you were chasing business in Ontario as suggested, but it is not okay in Quebec."

Martin was a persuasive guy. I was even starting to fall under his spell somewhat when Gerard saved me by threatening us. "Just so you know," he said menacingly, "there is a way out for you jokers, and that is to stay the fuck away from my customers."

"Or what?" Ken asked, deadpan.

"Or I will fucking destroy you!" hissed Gerard angrily.

Simon very calmly pulled his left hand in towards his right elbow and then in a blaze of action let it fly in a wicked backhanded slap that caught Gerard right between his mouth and his nose. His head flew back and crashed into the wooden booth divider behind him. It sounded like a double tap. There was maybe the same shock value too.

"Don't you threaten us again, old man," Simon told him evenly. It went deathly quiet in the restaurant.

Around our table, nobody said a word until the waitress came over a few seconds later with our food. She was startled to see that Gerard's nose was bleeding. He snatched his wrapped burger off her tray and leaned in towards Simon as he forced himself past. "You are going to regret that, my friend," he warned him through his thickening lips.

"Dude! Awesome!" I half-laughed nervously to Simon after Gerard and Martin had walked out.

Ken had a slight smile on his face, but I could see that he was preoccupied, maybe even worried. Perhaps wondering why it was, when we already had potential problems with the Albanian mafia, that we needed to stir up a fight with Quebec Air, too. He ate his burger contemplatively.

System Crash

To add insult to Quebec Air's injury, we received a call from Alain on his expensive satellite phone to ask us to take on their logging camp re-supply needs. Quebec Air had let him down again. We were delighted. We would now be flying almost every day. We had a bit of re-supply capacity left, but we wanted to make sure that we filled it with year round business. We were also keeping our weekends free to cater to some fly-in fishing trips. Our unique accommodation model meant that we could offer a coming-together party for the guys on the Friday night, catered by Tina. They would then stay over so we could fly them out really early on the Saturday morning without breaking a sweat. Pick-up would usually be arranged for Sunday afternoon.

It was on one such weekend fishing trip that the fun started.

We loaded up a party of six young, boisterous, but obviously well-to-do guys. They were nice enough, but their egos did seem to get in the way of everything. So even though it was early on a Saturday morning, they were all in high spirits, turning even their most mundane tasks into an alpha-male contest.

We took off on runway 09 and were making the initial climb over Lower Duck Island when the engine cut out. It simply died, going from 2,200 rpm one second to absolutely nothing the next. We were too low to even think about trying to restart. Simon had the captain's chair and he immediately went into stall recovery mode, forcing the yolk down to maintain forward momentum.

The boys in the back went silent. They could see that this was real trouble.

Luckily, we had not turned out yet so we were still pretty much lined up with the river. We decided to make an emergency landing on the far side of the Lower Duck. I had enough time to tell ATC that we were ditching and then we started going in. I turned around to the passengers behind me and said, "Brace! Take up a brace position. We're going in for an emergency landing!"

By the time I looked up, Simon had the plane about 100 feet above the water. We seemed to drop suddenly from that height and we hit the water with a tremendous splash. The force of the impact rattled us and the Otter tipped dangerously forward as it bow-waved to a stop. I was convinced that we'd broken the back of the aircraft. From the passenger compartment, there was a lone cheer as one of them realized that we had just survived.

A police boat pulled up alongside us ten minutes later, a RIB sporting big twin Mariner counter-screws running quietly. "Everybody all right? Anybody hurt in there?" called the patrolman.

I opened the side window and yelled back, "We're all okay, but we don't have any power. Can you tow us to the airport?"

We fixed their line onto the forward tie-points on top of the floats and let the RIB pull us back upstream to the airport. Simon called Ken and had him waiting for us on the ramp with the airport ramp-lifter. This ugly machine drove down the ramp and maneuvered two long steel arms either side of and beneath the Otter. The arms were connected to each other by belting so that when the arms were raised, forklift style, the floatplane, now resting on this belting platform, was lifted clean out the water. Then it drove noisily back up the ramp and deposited the Otter onto its wheels on the apron. The belting was then pulled clear from the one side of the contraption and the ramp-lifter drove off.

Our passengers were sad to have lost out on a fishing trip. They did appreciate, however, that they now had far bigger bragging rights – surviving a plane crash! They took a few photographs of us all standing solemnly around the grounded Otter. A couple of weeks later we would receive a framed one in the mail.

"It's that bastard Gerard," muttered Ken, furious. "He could have killed everyone!"

Simon and I weren't so sure. We all waited impatiently for the aircraft maintenance team to tell us what they'd found.

It took them a couple of hours to decide that there was nothing at all wrong with the engine itself. The problem was electrical. The master electrical circuit had been shut down, just as if the motor had been intentionally turned off. This was an old system. It didn't have the intelligence to detect that it was in mid-flight and to therefore override the engine kill instruction. They weren't even sure that an override could have been possible because the circuitry had been eaten through with a highly concentrated acid. The process would have taken maybe 30 seconds.

"So how the hell did that acid get there?" Ken demanded of the mechanic.

"I think you were sabotaged," he answered. "I found bits of glass in there. It might have been some sort of altitude sensitive device that released the acid when it detected an altitude change."

"Must have been pretty sensitive then," mused Simon, "we were barely at 1,000 feet."

The police came around and found the altitude bomb. They said it was probably East European, but really, anyone could have set it. We told them about Gerard and his threats and they went off to interview him.

It took two weeks to clean out the acid damage, do the engine and frame assessments, and put the Otter back together again. In that time, we chartered a third party service to do the weekly customer rounds to keep our business secure. The customers were happy and that was the main thing.

By the end of the first week, the police had been back to us to report that they didn't believe that Gerard had set the device. This left us feeling a little unsettled. Then surprisingly, Gerard himself turned up at our base to inform us, personally, that he had nothing whatsoever to do with the Otter incident. He admitted that he would not have lost a lot of sleep over our being put out of action, but as a fellow airman, he would never, ever intentionally fuck with someone else's ride. We believed him. Especially when he smiled at the end and told us that he was watching our progress with interest from now on. I guess he was rooting for the bad guys, whoever they were.

Without warning and quite out of the blue, we received a visit from Detective Sergeant Parry that weekend. He brought disturbing news.

Kickback

"I've been keeping a distant eye on you two," Parry told us. "I've had Mike watch the news wires for any mention of your names. I knew when you received your pilots licenses, when you registered your company, and so on. Then Mike came across the police report, suggesting aircraft sabotage, and I thought I had better come over and explain a few things to you."

"Don't tell me," I said quietly, "We didn't kill Alpha, did we? They're still out there, looking for revenge!"

"Almost right," Parry half agreed. "We think that we did get Alpha. Jasleen Luga was Alpha, not Egon, the husband. She must have been the one that leaked the stock tip to her father which started all the trouble. Perhaps a moment of weakness. Anyway, as I had suspected at the time, it turns out that Egon was indeed connected to the Albanian mafia. He was the younger son of one of the Albanian bosses." Parry let this sink in for a second before continuing.

"But contrary to what I had thought at the time," Parry mused, "we now believe that what Alpha were doing in Canada was independent of the father's mafia activities. The problem seems to be the family connection itself. Getting involved with killing the old man's son is what has gotten you two into trouble now. They clearly know who you are. They obviously also know where you are."

That last bit was chilling. As time had passed uneventfully since the shootings, we had allowed ourselves to believe that all the Alpha players were dead. This being the case, we figured it was no longer possible for the Albanian mafia to find out who we were, or what our involvement had been. That theory seemed to have come unraveled now and this was a real concern. It was tough to be brave when a foreign mafia organization wanted us dead. And they knew where we lived.

"Holy shit!" exclaimed Ken. Tina looked at him sharply. "Yes, well, I mean, we had better make a plan then," he added contritely.

"Yes, quite, agreed Parry. "A plan."

DS Parry stayed over with us that night. We fixed him up with one of the dormitory beds.

He was surprised to see how many people turned up for breakfast the next day. Very few of us old hands ever passed up Tina's breakfast. There were eight from NGE, four from Wolf, the four of us, and Parry himself.

A few months ago, Ken and Tina had rented out their Toronto house. Amongst the furniture that they kept was a massive mahogany table. This was now set up in our large dining room and it came with 18 seats.

Parry told us later that he hadn't realized how many lives might be endangered by an Albanian mafia attempt on the two of us. He was right. That issue forced him to rethink our security requirements, and ultimately, we benefited from a higher-end security system. Parry managed to get the whole set-up delivered, installed, and commissioned within ten days.

The Otter was already compromised. They had gotten access to it despite all the airport security. The logical thing to do was to store it at home under more controlled conditions. Parry called a few people and the next thing we knew, we were granted a river access ramp. The city did not want us keeping the Otter in the water lest it pollute or break free. However, we could take off and land on the aerodrome site and then taxi up to our ramp, and essentially haul the Otter onto our front lawn. A ramp was duly built, together with a winch and dolly system that Ken designed which made extraction and launching easy. A bonus feature was that we could winch the Otter all the way up to our warehouse, load it and relaunch it ready to go.

At the same time, Parry had a nine-foot diamond mesh steel fence erected around three sides of the property. This was a physical barrier designed as much to keep wildlife out as people. The front was left open to the river. A sliding security gate was placed across the driveway that could be opened and closed electronically to admit traffic.

Security lights were installed that lit the place up at night, inside the fence and up to the water. Parry also arranged a series of concealed laser beam and heat-sensed motion detectors around the yard, particularly covering the water frontage. When armed, a cold-blooded frog would have had difficulty moving around out there. Boss had to sleep inside.

The final perimeter was the house itself. All the windows and doors were alarmed with ingress and break detectors. This meant no more sleeping with the windows open, so we had to get the place air-conditioned too. Thankfully, we never did see the final bill for all this work.

Before he left at the end of the installation, Parry presented us each with a remote control fob. There was only one button on it. "Keep this on you at all times," he advised us. "Especially you, Tina, wear it around your neck. If you need help then you depress it three times in quick succession." He demonstrated the action. "It's linked to the master unit in your roof which will immediately summon the armed reaction unit of the RCMP. You can expect them to arrive in three minutes or less. Clear?"

Sleep came a little more easily after that. Plus we got the Otter re-certified and we could crack on and focus on business again.

Rapid Expansion

Ken convened our first board meeting. We elected him the first of our annually rotating Chairmen. We appointed our law firm as the corporate lawyer, confirmed the accountants, agreed on their fee, and signed the corporate banking arrangements. Then we read through the accounting report.

We had lost almost $100,000 in our first six months. Most of this was associated with our start-up: finding clients, aircraft running expenses, insurances, rents, depreciation and so on.

"But the bright side is that revenue is now $42,000 per month," said Ken. "So if we keep this up, we are on track for $500k annualized."

"That looks respectable," commented Simon. "Profit margins are still low, though. Projecting forward on our current basis, we would only be making $100,000 a year."

"Yes. I've been doing some thinking and I believe we can improve it significantly," said Ken. "With the Otter based here now, we save airport storage and overnight fees. The water landing fee is lower than using the runway. I have also found a cheaper insurance package, too. They like our new security system! So cost savings should add around $50,000 a year to our profits."

"Good stuff, Ken," I said. "You know, we are also starting to pick up a lot more market info regarding pricing and I reckon we could safely lift our prices by ten percent. We do after all, provide a significantly more augmented service package than straight forward re-supply."

"I'm with you, Eric, lets start talking to our customers about this," agreed Simon. "That could be another $50k."

We drew up personalized price increase letters and took these with us on our next re-supply runs. Our various customers appreciated our coming around and discussing this issue with them firsthand. They all agreed to the ten percent increase.

It had an unexpected effect, however. We started to receive a lot more inquiries from other camps in the area. We even had a few of their head office hotshots calling us, those that would not take our calls six months ago. We ignored those calls. It transpired that our competitors had heard of the successful implementation of our price increase. Not to be outdone, most of them had jumped onto this bandwagon and broadcast an increase of their own. The heavy handed manner in which they had attempted this, coupled with their inferior service to begin with, had chased many of those customers towards us. So, we cherry-picked those customers we could accommodate, but we still had about three times as much potential business as we needed.

"Let's charter," suggested Ken. So we chartered another Otter and took on the best of the rest of the customers. Simon and I split up so that we could each fly an Otter. We also short-term rented a house next door to take our overflow overnighters and Tina set about looking to hire some help.

Suddenly, we had doubled the size of the business. And it had taken a price increase to do this.

Michel, the geologist from Wolf pulled me aside one day as I was busy unloading the Otter with the help of his relief crew. I left them to it and followed him to the admin hut.

"You know that this is a JV, right?" he asked.

"Yes, you guys and the Chinese government," I responded.

"We're getting good sampling results. Now we're moving to

phase two. We need more people here. More drilling rigs. The Chinese are giving us *beaucoup* pressure to take some of their guys. They want them to learn." he told me.

I could see where this was heading and quickly assured him, "You were our first customer, Michel. We will do whatever we can to help you move more men and materials."

"Thank you, yes," he said ungrammatically, "but can you also accommodate Chinese at your house? They need special food, translation maybe, I don't know."

"When does it start?"

"The Chinook will bring the huts and drill rigs starting next week." he told me, "We can deploy them in two weeks, 20 of them."

"We'll be ready!" I assured him.

I told Ken and Simon about this new development over supper that night. Since I had already had half a day to think about it, I also had a partial solution.

We clearly needed both another aircraft and another pilot. Given the timing, we should hire the pilot and charter another Otter. We left Ken to run with that task.

We also needed more accommodation space. The second house was already full, which meant finding another one for the Chinese contingent. We left that to Tina.

The third component was that we needed additional warehousing space. The double garage was not doing it for us anymore. Our spare living room was already packed with stuff. I thought that one of those permanent fabric buildings would do the job. Another task for Ken.

Then we needed additional staff to clean and cook for our new guests. My suggestion was to get the girls to help find us some people to do all this, preferably two multi-taskers who could also translate for them if required. Thanks to the handover, most Hong Kong youngsters spoke Mandarin these days. So in case these new Mainlanders spoke no English, we would be ready for them.

Simon and Ken agreed with the plan. So the next day, being a Saturday, Simon and I blasted off on our bikes to Toronto to have a chat with the girls.

It went much better than we could have expected. Kelsey and Joy expressed an interest in doing this work themselves. Eva had found a job and the other two were at a loose end. It also meant that they could wind up their apartment sharing and Eva could go after the bachelor digs that she had her eye on. So they sorted their stuff out, bought two monster new backpacks, stuffed these with their personal things, and were ready to come away with us the next day.

We arrived back in Ottawa on Sunday evening. Ken couldn't believe it. We took the girls for a tour of the place. Tina got on famously with both of them. At the end of the tour, Kelsey wanted to know why we didn't just buy the farmland and build ourselves a new warehousing and accommodation block. None of us had considered that option. It was a good idea. We called the Realtor the next day and got her to explore the idea with the landlord.

The next evening, the Realtor came around with an offer to purchase. She told us that the landlord would sell for $850,000. After much discussion, we submitted an offer for $790,000. The landlord accepted it. Now, as if Ken didn't already have enough to do, he had to arrange a mortgage, get plans and permissions approved, and start putting our little empire together.

A few days later, we returned home to find Joe, a young-looking guy in his late 20s, waiting patiently for us in the office. He was short and muscular. His handshake made me wince and I could see that he hadn't meant it to. Ken made the introductions. This was a son of a friend, one who just happened to have a current commercial license to fly the de Havilland Otter DHC-3. He seemed like a nice enough guy.

"You can come with me tomorrow," offered Simon. "Then the next day, you can fly with Eric. We'll gladly check you out, see if you fit, and if you do, well then we'll see about making you a job offer. Okay?"

"That's great, Mr. Goode, thank you!" replied Joe enthusiastically.

We let him call us Mr. for the two-day trial. He turned out to be a competent pilot and a personable guy. He got on well with our customers and he was fit and strong enough to handle a plane-load of cargo on his own if necessary. We made him a proposition over one of Tina's dinners. Everyone seemed happy with it, so Joe became our first full-time employed pilot. He and Ken now had a week to find, test, and charter another Otter. Then we'd need to figure out how to shoehorn another floatplane onto our shrinking front lawn.

The mere fact that we needed to do this reminded me that the Albanian mafia was still out there and no doubt still after us. I was getting tired of being afraid. I wanted them to show themselves. Anything seemed preferable to the constant thought that they were waiting to ambush us somewhere. I wished we could just get on with it.

To be fair to Joe and to make sure he understood the risks, I told him the whole story. He listened quietly and took it all in stride. Clearly, not too much flustered Joe. I liked that about him.

Cash Cow

In between all this excitement, I picked up the newspaper at breakfast one morning and saw a familiar face staring back at me. It took quite a long time to place him. It was one of our plane crash survivors. I took the picture over to the wall and compared it with the framed shot of all of us standing around the Otter. Yup, he was in it. His name was Guy Barnes and he was dead.

The newspaper report informed us that Barnes was an entrepreneur in the telecommunications sector who had made millions as his company had taken off. He had been killed in a freak snowmobile accident in BC. His business partner had been with him and appeared to be quite distressed about it all.

"Shit, you survive a plane crash and then die like that?" mused Ken.

"Sounds a little suspicious to me," I said. "The business partner being there, and surviving it, makes me wonder."

"What are you getting at, dear Partner?" asked Simon.

Ken also joined in the ribbing, "Yeah, Partner, you got some simmering concerns that you want to murder us for?"

Joe was at the table, too. I suspect that in an effort to politely change the direction of the conversation he asked, "Do you think that the sabotage attempt on your Otter was actually the Albanians going after you two, or could it have been an earlier attack on this guy's life?"

I was grateful to Joe for the diversion. It also made us all stop and think.

"Joe has a point," Ken said. "The original logic could still be intact you know. Perhaps the Albanians really don't know who to go after. I mean, realistically, it's nearly two years since the Lugas were killed. Surely these guys would have taken you both out long ago. Plus, they could have done it without endangering other people."

"I like theory." I said. "I just wish that I could believe it. We've been living with this Albanian threat for so long now that it's hard to just dismiss it."

"Yeah," Simon agreed. "It's a part of us now. But you guys are right, it's also been over six months since the sabotage job. You'd think that if they were serious, they would have had another go since then. We should try hard to ignore them from now on. Maybe become a little more fatalistic, you know, what will be will be sort of thing."

We resolved to do just that. It was quite liberating and we responded by throwing ourselves wholeheartedly into the business of Bald Eagle Air Transportation Inc.

Ken proved to be a master expediter. He got the building plans approved, applied to re-zone the property for business and had all the interim permissions signed off in the meantime. After all, Ontario was desperate to get business moving again and we could demonstrate quite a solid performance. The buildings were completed in six months.

Just in case however, the security systems were extended and integrated into those that Parry had initially set up.

With three aircraft flying full-time and with a full guest house on the property, we were making good money. We moved out of the houses we had rented in the neighborhood and installed all the staff in our main house and all the guests in our new 20-room wing.

All the overflow supplies were moved to our large new combination garage/warehouse/workshop unit which Ken had designed. We let the girls redecorate the now-liberated living room. They managed to create a blend of high tech entertainment equipment, comfortable seating and of all things, a pool table.

We headed into full-blown summer that year making an annualized $360,000 profit from a $1.2 million turnover business. We didn't skimp on paying ourselves and our staff a living wage, either. Our only liability in the business was the mortgage and we paid down the capital component by $200,000 that year. Life was good.

Mission Critical

The chartered Otter which I usually flew was being serviced, so I was keeping Simon company on his rounds when Ken radioed us. He had received an urgent appeal for help from the Randville farming settlement pharmacist that we had met in our early days of drumming up business. There had been a shooting accident. Could we get there quickly and evacuate the victim to Ottawa?

"We are ten minutes away from our final drop at Cross Lake. It's close to Randville. We'll make that one fast and get going again ASAP," I told Ken. He replied with the GPS coordinates.

We put down at the lake, which was supposed to be our final stop, and quickly unloaded their supplies onto their newly constructed jetty. Their pile of sample boxes were waiting for us which we loaded up and strapped down in the Otter. We were on our way again in 15 minutes, both panting a little from the exertion. Simon punched in the coordinates and we headed directly for the settlement. It took about twelve minutes to touchdown on their grassy runway. The whole inbound journey time since we had received the distress call was less than 40 minutes.

The pharmacist was waiting with a small entourage. They all looked worried and were already starting to gather up the injured party for a quick transfer. As Simon turned the Otter around, I stepped into the rear, slid out, assembled, and locked in the one permanent stretcher that we had always kept available since the Wolf broken leg incident. Then I opened the door with the engine still running and we lifted the shot guy into the stretcher. The pharmacist came aboard too, shouting that he wanted to join us. I flipped down a seat for him against the rear bulkhead. Then I strapped the injured guy in and climbed back into my seat. "We're good to go," I told Simon as I put on my headset.

We made it back in 85 minutes, assisted by a useful tailwind and a heavy hand on the throttle. O/R was on form again, clearing us straight in to an ambulance waiting for us on the apron. We made the transfer and the pharmacist got into the ambulance too and it disappeared. We left the Otter at Rockcliffe for the night and got a lift with Ken for the short ride back to BEAT HQ.

"Any idea who the injured guy was?" Simon asked Ken.

"Jacques du Rand. He's the only son of the richest woman in the area. She has an interest in virtually all the farms and owns all the businesses in the settlement," explained Ken. "There was a terrible drought in the mid-1990s which effectively bankrupted the whole area. Old Madame Du Rand stepped in, bought up the businesses, and bankrolled something like 90 percent of the farmers. She gave them a choice: pay the loan back with low interest or swap it for a 25 percent stake in their farms." Smart woman, I thought. Ken continued, "Most chose the equity option. They like her, trust her and know that she could step in with more money if they hit another lousy year. Mme. du Rand is quite the legend over there. Her son has been steadily taking over the business reigns because the old lady is getting frail. Still sharp as a tack though from what they say."

"What about the son?" I asked, "Is he a good guy, too?"

"I don't know. I googled him before I came over to the airport. He's a quiet one. For all the family wealth, he sure keeps his head below the social radar. About all I know is that he graduated with an Agricultural and Environmental Sciences degree from McGill."

McGill was in Montreal and consistently one of Canada's top five universities.

"Anyway," said Ken, "I doubt that the du Rands will have difficulty paying our invoice."

Decision Gateway

We met Jacques du Rand two weeks later. He had called Ken and asked us for a ride back to the farm. He arrived by taxi at BEAT HQ together with his minder, the pharmacist. Jacques was a few years older than Simon and I. They were both very gracious and very thankful for our quick evacuation to Ottawa. I piggybacked them home together with supplies for Alain's logging camp. Jacques sat in the co-pilot's seat, which was a real thrill for him, for two takeoffs and landings. It also allowed us to chat through the headsets once I had the Otter flying straight and level.

"So, how did you get shot?" I asked him, eventually

He looked like he wasn't happy to answer that one, but after a few moments of staring at me he said, "I think it was a warning. The police are not so sure."

"Wow, a warning for what?"

"Our farming lands are underlain with very rich copper deposits," explained Jacques "I think there are many companies out there who want it."

"Who owns the mineral rights?" I asked him.

"We do. We own the Exploration Rights. They are valid for two years at a time and are renewable with proof of minimal exploration expenditure. We also own the Extraction Rights, or the mining lease. This also requires that we do some work, make quarterly statistics submissions, and so forth. It's costing us maybe $10,000 a year all in, which we think of as a small price to pay to keep the whole area mine free."

"Why do you want to do that?" I asked.

"We're organic farmers," he explained. "This comes with a certain commitment to the local ecology. All of our agricultural activities always seek a balance with the environment. Some of our early French forefathers took wives from the local *Anishinabeg*, so we also have some deep-rooted beliefs in our culture, which favor excessive nature over excessive industry." He paused before continuing, "Of course, we would be happy with a harmonic balance, but we distrust the mining companies. We see too much corporate greed, and the worst manifestation of their greed is the pollution they leave behind."

I asked, "Aren't there good environmental protection laws in Canada, though?"

"Yes, but there's pitifully little policing and enforcement of those laws. The mining companies know this, so they cut all sorts of corners. Until this situation improves, we are not allowing any mining on our properties." he informed me, matter-of-factly.

"So why you? Why did you get shot?" I wanted to know.

"They see me as their main opposition," said Jacques with a shrug. "With me out of the way, they'll go to work on my mother until she signs something that she shouldn't have. It's taking all my powers of persuasion to stop her conceding right now. She wants her son safe, and she's not in good health herself." Jacques sighed. "And no, I can't prove a thing. I didn't even see the shooter, just felt it whack me from behind. Then nothing."

"Well good thing you survived, my friend," I told him with renewed respect.

The driver of the SUV she had sent for her son informed me that Mme. du Rand insisted that I join her and Jacques for lunch. I was both hungry and curious, so I closed up the Otter and climbed into the vehicle. The driver took us up to the only high ground in the area. It was well screened with trees, but when we got up there, we were greeted with the sight of a magnificent stone-built home. The majestic house sat on two acres of lawned garden with shade trees and elegant flowers. It would be a completely different picture in the winter, but right now it was breathtaking.

Mme. du Rand was waiting for us on her veranda. She was tall and gray-haired with piercing blue eyes. She hugged Jacques and fussed about him, wanting to know everything there was to know about his injury, its current status, and its prognosis. She eventually turned to me and introduced herself. "Thank you for getting here so quickly after the shooting," she said. "I have been told that if it wasn't for your airplane, he would have died. As it was, he was almost dead when they found him." She shuddered. "Come inside, Eric. Chef has prepared Jacques' favorite lunch."

"No way! Chicken curry?" laughed Jacques happily.

It was delicious. "He spent a year in England after graduating," explained Mme. du Rand, as we sat at the table. "They taught him all about curry and beer over there."

I could see that Madame du Rand was just so happy and so relieved to have her son back. He clearly meant the world to her, and I could fully understand how an aggressive mining company might use this to bully her into relinquishing her mineral rights. I was pleased that Jacques was back in the saddle, but there would no doubt be some tense discussions between the two of them in the days to come.

After lunch, Jacques went to lie down and Mme. du Rand and I sat on the veranda enjoying a coffee before I left.

"You have a magnificent house, Madame," I told her.

"Thank you. My husband, Jacques Senior, was the third du Rand generation to be born here. He knocked down the old house and had this one built. I love it."

The SUV drove up, so I left the *grande* old dame sitting there and went back to the strip with the driver. Before he drove away, he produced a check already made out to Bald Eagle Air Transportation Inc. for the full invoice value. Boy, no wonder people liked the du Rands around here.

Corporate Ethics

Flying home from Randville, I thought a lot about ethics. I was worried that we were servicing companies that under certain circumstances, would stoop to murder. What did that say about us? What did this say about the mining companies? I looked at every mine and every exploration camp through different eyes now. We were going to have to think about this as a team and get our strategy sorted out.

After I had landed on the river, I taxied up to our ramp and positioned the Otter between the guides which brought me over the dolly and snugged me up against the float stops. Ken had built a partially-submerged folding gate at the back of the guides that allowed the aircraft into the lift space, but would not let it float out again. This gave us all the time we needed to shut the airplane down, do whatever else was required on board, then still get out, secure the aircraft to the dolly and activate the winch, all single-handedly.

I walked up next to the Otter as the winch hauled it right up to the warehouse. Then I chocked the dolly wheels, unclipped the winch cable and pulled the cable back to our dock. Near the dock I pulled the next dolly in line out from its storage position 90 degrees from the winch track, clipped it to the cable and pushed it into the water. It came to rest when the cable went taut. I activated the winch and got the dolly positioned just right for the next Otter. This was our standard procedure.

Then I went inside to wait for Simon.

As it turned out, he was next in line. He got his aircraft safely out the water and made ready the last dolly for Joe. I called Simon and Ken both into the lounge. We each got a beer and I told them the story of Jacques' brush with death and his theory behind it. Then I went into my ethical concerns. Simon was pensive, thinking. Ken took a different road.

"That's conjecture, Eric," he retorted. "We can *not* be giving up good business because we *think* that our customers are dirty. And by the way, which of the four or five mining companies that we deal with do we think is the dirty one? Is it any of them? It's an impossible call to make. I say we leave things as they are. Let's not mess with a winning formula."

"What do you think, Simon?" I asked him.

"I hate bullies, as you know, and I think that what this company is doing is tantamount to bullying. The bullies could realistically only be Wolf Copper. They are the dominant copper miner on the ground, and we've caught them conniving before. I say let's drop them," said Simon. "I agree with Eric, we must take a stand on this."

"Look," Ken said, "I agree that BEAT needs to take a stand against corruption and extortion, but we don't have the proof. Your proposed action is premature. We need proof."

"Okay, Ken, if we get irrefutable proof that one of the mining companies *is* squeezing the du Rands, would you agree with me now that we dump them as a customer?" I asked.

"Yeah, I'd go with that," agreed Ken. I resolved to keep my eyes open from now on.

Soon after that internal discussion, I found myself doing the Wolf JV re-supply run to Cross Lake. I unloaded their supplies onto the jetty and picked up a few sample boxes which had been left for me. I would ordinarily get going again straight away. However, today was a single destination day and I had the time, so I made my way down the jetty to find Michel. He was in the admin hut with one of the Chinese foremen that frequented our guest house. "Hurro Elic!" called the Chinese guy happily, getting his consonants all fouled up.

"*Ni Hao,* Wei Ming," I replied, thus exhausting my Mandarin. "Hi Michel. How is your coffee supply today?"

"It's good, my friend," came Michel's reply. "Let me just finish up targeting his next exploration holes, then he can go to work," he said, indicating Wei Ming. "Help yourself to some coffee."

I did just that, and after Michel dismissed Wei Ming, he indicated that we go outside. They had built a very rough outdoor dining area under the trees and we took our coffee there.

The proximity of the Wolf JV made it the closest of our mining customers to the Randville settlement. I pretended to be interested in the Wolf JV growth prospects for our own capacity planning purposes. What I really wanted to know was what they knew of the deposit below Randville and what their intentions were in that regard. We chatted around the subject a lot. I never did get a sense that Michel was aware that the Randville area held great promise.

Wolf was already confirmed not to be the most ethical of companies. They had stiffed their Chinese JV partner before in order to participate in a more lucrative option in Chile. They had also then appeared to cheat their Chilean partner out of joint control of their Punto Lanza JV. Notwithstanding these dirty tricks, I left Cross Lake feeling a lot happier that Michel appeared not to be complicit in anything untoward up in Randville. If anything, it was probably those corporate head office types. At least this murky behavior explained what must be keeping them so busy that they had no time to answer their goddamn phones.

~~~

PART FIVE : BLACK KNIGHT

CHAPTERS

Offshoring
Delegation
Third Party Logistics
Knowledge Transfer
Hostile Takeover
Open Communications
Contract Negotiations
Shotgun Clause
Dry Hole
Trojan Horse
Push-back
Exit Strategy

Offshoring

Kalem Luga was let out of his jail cell at exactly 2 p.m. He had spent the last six years in the high security facility in the Appenine mountains southwest of Bologna in northern Italy. He had been a model prisoner, never once retaliating when the notoriously cruel guards goaded him, never getting involved in a fight with an inmate, never doing or saying a thing that would lengthen his sentence.

He was taken to the main prison square where a dark blue sedan awaited him. The sedan was an Alpha Romeo with steel mesh partitioning off the back seat from those in front. There were no controls in the back for windows and doors, either.

The prison warden approached him and told him in Italian that he, Kalem Luga, had served his EU-mandated sentence and that as a consequence, he was now being deported back to his native Albania. He would be taken to Bologna airport and handed into the custody of an Albanian policeman waiting for him on board the scheduled Albanian Airlines flight to Tirana.

Luga got into the car and it sped out the gate. It kept going at high speed, blue light flashing through the mountain switchbacks until it joined the A1 *Autostrade*. Then turning northwards, the jailers gunned it all the way to the A14 split and followed that straight in to the Guglielmo Marconi Bologna-Borgo-Panigale airport. As they approached, the jailers got onto their radio and passworded themselves into the secure area. They drove right up to an Albanian Airlines Tupolev Tu-134. The passenger steps were still attached to the aircraft and the jailers stopped the Alpha Romeo directly alongside the foot of these steps. They pulled Luga out of the back seat and hustled him up the stairway. At the head of the steps waited a uniformed member of the Albanian State Police. He spoke briefly to the Italian jailers, signed some papers, then took his prisoner by the arm and guided him inside the

airplane. They sat in the first row on the left and with Luga
safely handcuffed to the window seat armrest, flight LV227
took off on schedule at 4:00 p.m.

As the wheels lifted off the tarmac of runway 12, Kalem Luga
let out a deep, audible sigh. His police escort tapped him
reassuringly on the back of his left hand. "Not long now, Sir"
he said.

Luga spent the 55 minute flight becoming quietly enraged. He
had attended his son's marriage to the beautiful Indian girl in
Toronto seven years ago. Then he had gone home for a short
spell before taking that trip to Zürich. He had arranged for the
proceeds of the Norwegian heist to be safely cleaned up and
transferred into the Swiss bank account. That had taken a few
weeks of careful work. Then he had driven out of Switzerland
as a precaution against the rigorous Swiss airport immigration
procedures.

He had been planning to take this very flight home when he
had been randomly selected at the Italian border. They had
targeted him initially because he was an Albanian, of course.
But they soon realized who it was they had caught. They had
tried to pressure him to admit to the Norwegian job, but they
were amateurs. Nobody understood pain and discomfort like
the Albanians. They would never break him. And they did not.

The cause of all his legal trouble was the fake Italian EU
passport in his bag. He hadn't even used it! That had cost him
six years in this shit-house country.

More importantly, it had prevented him from burying his son.
A father should never die before his son to begin with, but for
it to happen and then for his son to be denied a properly-
attended funeral was unthinkable. He pounded the armrest. The
bastards will pay! He had no idea yet who was responsible, but
whoever it was would intensely wish they were dead. And they

would die all right. Except they would beg for it to come much, much sooner. Their pain would wash away the insult to the family of Kalem Luga. It was the deepest of insults. It would therefore be the deepest of pain.

The Tupolev made good time and touched down on schedule on runway 18 at the Mother Teresa International Airport in Tirana, Albania. The noise of the reverse thrust roared through the cabin, drowning out some premature clapping, which started up again in earnest once the engine quietened down.

After the doors were opened, the State Policeman leaned over and unlocked Luga's handcuffs. He slipped them into his breast pocket, then extending his hand in a friendly handshake said, "Welcome home Mr. Luga." Then he stood up, smiling, and ushered him out and down the stairway to the waiting bus. They filled the bus up to save on a second journey and it groaned over to the Tirana International Arrivals building. People rushed out to get into line for immigration. Luga stood back to one side, then walked inside with the policeman.

In a few minutes a well-dressed official came out of a side office and beckoned the policeman over. Luga followed as the policeman entered the office.

"Welcome home, Mr. Luga!" said the official, with feeling. "Your car is waiting outside for you."

That's better, thought Luga. Respect. He nodded and walked out through the opposite door into the arrivals hall without saying a word. He saw his older son at once. Tears came to both of their eyes as they embraced for a long time.

"How is your mother?" inquired Luga senior as they disengaged.

"She is well, *baba*. She waits eagerly at home for your return," came the reply.

Outside, parked in front of a line of bright yellow taxis, stood a
black Mercedes ML350. It reflected regally off the new glass
walls of the terminal. Both Lugas got into the back seats and it
sped off, initially towards the city, then curling away and
heading into the Balkan uplands. They followed the Terkuzes
river through orchards, olive groves, and fields before heading
up a steep dirt road onto a prominent hill overlooking the
Adriatic coastline, 35 kilometers away to the west. On top of
this hill was the Luga compound, a spectacular clash of high
tech meets Ottoman fortress.

The ML swooped into the compound with guards scrambling
to open the gates at the last minute and closing them
immediately afterward. The boss was back and he did not
tolerate sloppiness.

Delegation

After a night spent eating, drinking and talking to his family, Kalem Luga was up early and jogging around the compound. Men watched him carefully from a discreet distance and through the security system cameras. He was back, showered and enjoying his breakfast when his older son, Afrim, made it down the stairs.

"You are growing fat, my *bir*," admonished the senior Luga quietly. "Tomorrow you will start to run with me in the morning."

"Yes, *baba*," said his son.

"This morning I wish to meet with my senior team," continued Luga, "Arrange this for ten thirty."

"They are already assembled in the compound and waiting for your call, father," replied Afrim.

"Good."

At half past ten a group of five men entered Kalem's giant office on the first floor. It had floor-to-ceiling glass windows overlooking the valley below and on to the Adriatic. It was said that these windows could withstand an RPG strike. There were lots of smiles, hugs and softly spoken greetings of great affection. Eventually Kalem got them seated around a long, rectangular boardroom table.

The tabletop was a continuous eight-inch-thick plank, cut from a single, massive Indonesian hardwood tree. The edging still featured the original bark, now varnished securely in place. The great table dominated the right-hand one-third of the room. The left-hand third of the room contained sofas and easy chairs arranged in a loose square. The central third was commanded by an imposing desk, the surface of which was again made from a solid eight-inch-thick piece of the identical hardwood.

"My mind is consumed with thoughts of vengeance for my son Egon's death," began Kalem quietly. "In the last two years of my prison sentence, I have thought of nothing else. I am unable even to concentrate on business." He was being surprisingly candid, even amongst this, his most trusted group.

There were lots of understanding nods and murmurs.

"So I have decided as follows," declared Kalem. "My son Afrim will continue to run the business affairs of the Luga Family. You will all report to him, just as you have done for the last six years. I will find the time to mentor Afrim in those areas that he needs it, but I think he has done a good job for me so far." Afrim glowed with pride and gratitude.

"Meanwhile," continued Kalem, "I intend to take my revenge on Egon's killers. This will put Egon's soul to rest and help me put my mind at ease. Only then can I come back to the business, God willing."

"God willing," the members murmured.

"Go now. Let my cleansing begin."

The men filed out. Kalem stood and walked to his desk. He picked up the framed photograph of his two boys and kissed Egon's image as a tear rolled down his cheek. Then he placed it gently at arms length 45 degrees to the right near his secure telephone. He sat and let out a deep breath before picking up the phone and dialing a number from memory. Kalem spoke to a man he referred to simply as *Gjahtar*. Hunter. They spoke for some time. Kalem's voice trembled with emotion and he could feel the rage building again. He finished the call with a barely-controlled instruction.

"Just bring them here to me, *Gjahtar*. Make sure they are unhurt. I want all the pain to happen in front of my eyes. My sanity depends on this!"

Third Party Logistics

Traveling to Canada from Albania is not so easy. The Hunter, however, was a practiced hand. He was also equipped with a real EU passport, which unlike Kalem's fake, was not going to set off any alarms.

The Hunter boarded an Albanian Airlines flight to Zürich and spent a few days there. He used the time to arrange a good deal of Canadian dollars and book a fresh return ticket from Zürich to Toronto.

It was late on Tuesday morning when he got back to Zürich Airport and made his way to the Air Canada check-in desks upstairs. The check-in agent looked at his passport, checked the details against her booking record, and printed off his first class ticket, seat 2K. She fixed a baggage sticker through the handle of his suitcase. It had a Star Alliance Priority Baggage identification protruding from it at an angle.

The Hunter knew from long experience that other than in the Far East, this was about the most useless piece of paper used by any airline. The priority in most cases was to make the passenger feel special at check-in. He nonetheless thanked the smiling agent, went through the line-up at security, and eventually got through immigration beyond that. He had an hour to kill in the Star Alliance First Class Lounge. He leaned back, closed his eyes and thought again about how he would go about his considerable task.

It was soon time to board. The Hunter gathered his belongings and walked to the gate. As he stepped aboard flight AC897 to Toronto, he was shown to the front right-hand side of the plane. They had new lie-flat seats installed in a herringbone pattern. It was comfortable enough. The flight departed on time and arrived ten minutes late at 4:30 p.m. local time in Toronto. The Hunter had slept all the way, avoiding conversations with any of the Air Canada crew. He pulled the shade open to bright sunshine. It always felt wrong, but he forced his mind to accept the jet-lag.

Immigration was long winded. He queued for 45 minutes. The only benefit to his first class ticket was that he was able to beat most of his own flight to the line. He still found himself behind all the flights that had landed before him. A flight from New Delhi was ahead of him and this was going through very slowly, the Canadians on high alert for potential over-stayers. When he got to the control point, the harried immigration officer demanded his return ticket, landing form, and passport. When he saw that the ticket was from Zürich and the passport was an EU issue, he became a little more polite.

"What brings you to Canada?" he wanted to know.

"Visiting friends and sight seeing."

"Where do your friends live?"

"Ontario," said the Hunter, "Missi...Missor," he faked.

"Mississauga," the immigration guy finished for him.

"That's the place," laughed the Hunter, establishing an early rapport.

"How long are you staying?" asked the immigration guy.

"Three weeks," answered the Hunter.

The immigration guy checked that the return flight gelled with this date, scribbled a code onto his landing form and handed the whole lot back. "Welcome to Canada." he said.

Despite the long wait at immigration, the baggage had still not arrived off the Zürich flight. The Hunter waited 15 minutes. By then he had been joined at the carousel by a dozen fellow first class travelers. At last, the luggage started to emerge. The first 20 bags had no priority stickers on them. Then magically, his battered suitcase popped out. It didn't even have any frequent flier brag tags on it. His first class colleagues didn't like that injustice at all.

With his case now on an airport trolley, the Hunter joined another line, this one snaking through customs. The New Delhi flight ahead of him had fouled that line up, too. Every customs agent was occupied searching luggage, asking loud questions and incredulously extracting anything from grandma's home-made *acha* to boxes of fresh, green mangoes. When he eventually made it to the head of the line, the Hunter was waved straight through. He sought out a taxi and gave the cabbie instructions to take him to the Four Seasons Hotel on Bloor.

The Hunter made a call to Philadelphia from a pay phone in the Four Seasons lobby. He spoke Albanian to a member in the Organization. The member gave him a public parking garage address in Toronto and a bay number. It was within easy walking distance.

The Hunter approached the parking garage carefully. He stopped outside and waited until he was sure that he was safe to proceed. He entered the high rise parking lot and took the elevator to the fifth floor. In the northeast corner was bay number 562 and parked in it was a newish Hyundai Tucson SUV. It had Ontario plates and was an everyday silver color. He walked all around the parking garage as if looking for his car. He found no obvious traps, so he walked confidently up to the driver's side and pulled on the front door handle. The door opened. No alarms sounded. The Hunter got in.

The Tucson was the V6 version. It was clean inside. He found that the right-hand side armrest opened up, revealing a storage box below it. In the box were the keys, a 13mm flat head spanner and the parking entrance ticket. The Hunter tried the ignition, it was dead. He popped the hood, got out and saw that the battery had been disconnected. He reconnected the positive terminal using the spanner and this sounded the car alarm. He quickly shut that off with the remote control fob and the SUV returned to its ready mode. It started right away this time. It cost him $20 to get the ticket validated in the auto-pay machine, then he drove it around to his hotel and parked it in their parking garage.

The Hunter opened the rear door which hinged upwards. In the luggage space floor, there was a panel. He lifted the latch and raised the panel. It covered a removable compartment organizer, like a large printer's tray, designed to hold various tools, hazard markers, a first aid kit, and so on. Below this organizer lay the spare, and wrapped in the well of the spare wheel was a Glock G19 compact 9mm pistol, fully loaded with its maximum 15 rounds. There were also two spare magazines, both full, and a plain manila envelope.

The Hunter stuffed the weaponry into his pants pockets and opened the envelope. It contained one six-by-eight-inch photograph of a man standing outside a building taking a puff from a cigarette. The date and time were printed onto the corner of the photograph. It was dated a week ago and the time stamp said 10:55 a.m. Written on the back of the photograph were the words "Detective Sergeant Parry, Ontario Securities Commission, 20 Queens Street West". Turning the photo over, the Hunter saw that there was enough of the building visible that he would easily be able to recognize it.

Next, the Hunter looked for the local telephone number. It was in the car manual jacket, disguised as a towing service. He called this from the lobby payphone and spoke in Albanian to the woman who answered. "Just a moment," she said.

A man's voice came on a minute later, "Yes?" he inquired carefully.

The Hunter thanked him for the vehicle and the package. He asked if he could get someone to help him in the next few days and the answer was affirmative, just call.

The Hunter took himself off for a good meal at the hotel restaurant and an early night. He had much to achieve in the days ahead.

Knowledge Transfer

After breakfasting in his room the next day, the Hunter got a map from the concierge desk and walked down to the address scribbled on the photograph. He found it easily enough, noting that it was an entrance to a major shopping mall. He observed how the area near the entrance was where people came outside to smoke. He found a coffee shop that allowed him to watch this spot and he sat there nursing a latte for an hour before the man in the photograph showed up, leaned against the glass wall, and lit a cigarette. It was 10:50 a.m. Parry went back in again just before 11:00 a.m.

The Hunter had a look around inside the mall. He spotted the bank of elevators and he found Parry's place of employment, the OSC, listed on the 19th floor.

OK, he thought, this will be at least a two-man job. He called his local contact from one of the shopping center pay-phones. They set it up for the next day.

In the morning, the Hunter met with Aasif, his local Organization contact. They rode together to the shopping mall, Aasif driving. The idea was to drive past while Parry was having a smoke. The Hunter checked his weapon and stuck it in his back pocket. Then they drove west along Queen Street, timing it just right.

There was a pedestrian traffic light right where Parry usually stood. Aasif drove up to the light and stopped. It was still green and the driver immediately behind him started honking his horn impatiently. The Hunter got out of the passenger side, walking briskly around the back of the Tucson. The honking driver mistook this for some aggressive retaliation and peeled hard left into the moving traffic with a squeal of tires.

The Hunter continued walking fast around the back of the SUV towards the doorway. Halfway there, he seemed to notice Parry and stopped. Then he shouted, "Hey, Parry! Get over here, we got some serious shit going down!" Parry looked surprised. "Come on Detective Sergeant, move!" shouted the Hunter, raising his voice above the noise of the traffic. Parry came off the wall dropping his almost finished cigarette and moved towards the idling Tucson. The Hunter turned around and hurried back to the SUV. He opened the back door and said, "Quickly, get in, all hell's breaking loose over there."

"What? Where?" Parry was confused. How did this guy know him? What was going on? In his confused state, he got into the SUV and the Hunter got in beside him, forcing him to scoot over. Aasif gunned the engine, moving quickly down Queen Street. "What's the problem?" Parry asked more sensibly, "And who are you guys?"

"We're your worst nightmare, Parry," said the Hunter, pulling his pistol out and pointing it at Parry. "Put your hands on your head. Do it right now." His tone left no room for argument. Parry put his hands on his head and the Hunter snapped cuffs on him, singlehandedly threading the cuffs through the back seat headrest at the same time. He had clearly done this before. Then he leaned over and extracted Parry's gun from its shoulder holster. He patted him down, lifted his trouser cuffs, and discovered Parry's mousegun. "Nice," he said, pocketing it. He also found Parry's wallet and phone. He tossed both out the window.

"What's this about?" asked Parry.

The Hunter stared him in the eye and said, "If you make another sound, I'll shoot you in the knee." It was clear that the Hunter meant every word. Parry shut up.

Aasif drove the three of them to his house in Scarborough. By Scarborough standards it was a pretty ordinary house, except that it had an attached garage, which Aasif opened with the remote controller in his pocket. Once the garage door had closed again, Aasif unlocked the back doors of the SUV and the Hunter got out and stretched. He walked around to Parry's door, opened it, and leaned in. He found the release button for the headrest and pulled the entire unit out of its sockets, releasing Parry's handcuffed hands from behind the back of his head. Parry looked relieved to have his hands in front of him again.

Aasif pointed them towards a door at the rear of the garage that led into a part of the basement. This area had once been used as an underground wine cellar. The pigeon-hole cabinetry, once holding a vast collection of wine, stood empty along the walls of the cellar. Aasif was indeed a good Muslim.

"Did you get the items I requested?" asked the Hunter in Albanian.

"Yes Sir," Aasif confirmed, pointing towards the shadows at the rear of the cellar.

"Okay, Aasif, thank you. You should go now. Close the door tightly on the way out. Take your wife somewhere far away where she won't hear the screaming," he suggested pleasantly.

"Yes, Sir." Aasif was going to do exactly that.

"On your knees, Parry!" the Hunter said, suddenly in English. Parry complied quickly. "Hands out!" He did that too. The Hunter retrieved a set of ankle chains and a steel cable from the shadows. He clicked the chains onto Parry's ankles. The steel cable had hooks fastened to both ends. The Hunter hooked one end through the links between Parry's handcuffs and passed the cable around a stud in the wall, in front of Parry, close to the floor. He pulled on the loose end and the cable went taut, threatening to pull Parry face forward onto the basement floor.

Then the Hunter took the loose end to the opposite wall behind Parry. He repeated the procedure in reverse, passing the cable first around a stud near the floor then hooking it into the chains between Parry's feet. He pulled on both loose ends now and Parry went down, prone, face into the floor. He couldn't cushion the impact in any way.

The Hunter went back to the shadows and fetched an old-fashioned fence ratchet. He attached the grippers to the recently-pulled cables at either end and started ratcheting them together. The effect was to stretch Parry between the studs until he could no longer move. After this, the Hunter returned to the shadows one last time. He came back with a steel anvil, the type one might shape horseshoes with, and a four pound hammer. He set the anvil underneath the fingers of Parry's right hand.

Parry started to hyperventilate. He knew that this was going to end badly for him and he was completely helpless and alone. Parry heard some rustling of plastic, then he heard the man with the strange accent say "Look up, Parry!" He did, with some trepidation. He had just enough time to see the man, now wearing some sort of plastic raincoat, raise a hammer above his head and bring it down with full force onto his pinky finger. The shock drove a million volts through his arm. He saw his finger explode and the raincoat spatter with blood. Then he felt the pain and he screamed. He was still screaming as he passed out. He woke up again, screaming, as the man continued to pour water over his head to revive him. The pain was indescribable. His entire being was taken up with trying to deal with it. He felt himself passing out again and he willed the blackness to come.

The Hunter looked down at Parry. He was still bucking, thrashing, and screaming. Thankfully, they could not be heard from the street, but even if some noise got out, this neighborhood was rough enough that it would probably pass unnoticed. He watched as Parry passed out again from the pain. He picked up his bucket of water and revived him, as he had already done several times in the last 15 minutes.

Although Luga had asked that he not hurt the killers, the Hunter needed to know who else, if anyone, was involved in this affair. In order for this to work, his experience was that the person being asked the questions should first understand extreme pain, should second understand that the Hunter had no qualms about inflicting it and third, should understand that it was inversely proportional to telling the truth. Objectives one and two had been met here. He would have to wait for Parry's brain to recover before he could finish the task.

"Parry, do you hear me?" the Hunter asked him. Parry's screams had turned to sobs. His brain was starting to function again. "Speak to me, Parry, or I start on the next finger!"

"No...please...Christ...pain," sputtered Parry.

"Okay, Detective Parry. I believe that I have your attention, now, correct?"

"Yes, whatever you want, aah Christ that hurts! Tell me what you want. Please. I'll help you."

The Hunter was quite sure that Parry would shoot his own mother in this state. "I want to know three things, Parry, you listening?" he asked.

"Yes, for fuck sake, yes!" blurted Parry. He was still in a world of pain.

"Profanity does not impress me, Parry. Pain thresholds impress me. I like to test those."

"I'm sorry. I'm so sorry. I'm in such pain. Forgive me." blubbed

Parry.

"Okay, the first thing I want to know are the names and whereabouts of your immediate family. Go." said the Hunter.

"My ex-wife is in Florida. Her name is Laura Parry. We had no children. My mother, Jane, and father, Clarence Parry are both deceased." He looked up briefly, grimacing with pain at the movement. "They are in the Mount Pleasant cemetery. My brother James is in Japan teaching English. I have his address somewhere but I don't know if it's still valid. He moves around a lot. I don't have any sisters."

The Hunter stared at him a long time, saying nothing.

"Please, it's all true," said Parry sincerely.

"Question two," said the Hunter at length, "I want to know the names and whereabouts of all of the members of the team that contributed in any way to the killing of Egon Luga."

"I...you can't ask me that...surely?" said Parry, distressed even through the pain.

"Wrong answer!" barked the Hunter and brought the hammer down hard on what remained of Parry's pinkie.

Parry opened his mouth to scream but no sound came out, just silent, shocking waves of pain. His arm turned white hot as the shattered, exposed nerves in his finger tip transmitted the assault back to his brain. He blacked out again, mercifully.

The Hunter looked at the stub of finger. It had burst like a firecracker. Bits of bone protruded. He thought he could see raw nerve endings. It had started to bleed again so this last hammer blow had resulted in major blood spatter. He looked across at the tiny video camera mounted on its little tripod. The lens seemed clear of blood and mess.

It took Parry considerably longer to come out of this trauma. When he did, he was shaking from the shock and the pain.

"Are you ready to give me the right answer, Parry?" asked the Hunter.

"I did it...I killed Egon...in his car..." Parry was flaking in and out of consciousness.

"If you killed him in his car, you must have had help," said the Hunter.

"They're only ana...analysts, not cops...Egon and the dirty cop captured us. I killed Egon. I'm your man."

"So who killed the cop?"

"Eric...no me, I killed the cop too," there was real pleading in his eyes, "You must believe me."

"One more time, Parry. What are their names and where are they now?"

Parry's head dropped forward and hit the floor with a dull thud. He groaned and said something. He was crying. Great, big, heaving sobs.

"Repeat that, Parry!" said the Hunter sharply.

Parry seemed to get himself under control. He looked up, tears streaking his pain wracked face, "Eric Hanson and Simon Goode, they're in Ottawa, I don't know where exactly. They were only analysts!" His head pitched forward again, spent.

"Question three," began the Hunter. At this, Parry broke down completely. He could take very little more. "Question three, Parry," the Hunter repeated after a while, "Are you repentant, truly remorseful and sorry that you took the life of Egon Luga?"

"I am, yes," said Parry. He looked it too. Sorry that he had ever stuck his nose into this terrible mess.

"Tell Egon's father. Tell him how sorry you are," said the Hunter pointing at the camera.

"I'm sorry, Mr. Luga. I apologize for your son's death," whimpered Parry.

The last thing Parry heard was the snick of his own mousegun before the Hunter shot him through the temple with it. The exit wound spattered the video lens. The Hunter walked around the back of the camera and lifted it up from behind. He switched it off, cleaned it up, and dropped it into his pocket. Then he wiped down everything he'd touched, put it all into a garbage bag, and went upstairs to the garage. He found the bucket of water waiting for him and used it to wash up. Then he hit the wall switch for the garage door, got into the SUV and set the GPS to go to the Four Seasons.

He whistled along to a happy radio tune as he drove back.

Back in his room, he downloaded the digital video onto his laptop. He burned this onto a DVD, and placed the DVD inside a hardcover book that he had brought with him. Opening the book to the inside cover, he wrote in *Albanian*, "My brother, I am sorry that this one was not returned to you in person. I had a difficult choice. I trust the film makes up for your disappointment." He packed the book into a yellow kraft bubble envelope and addressed it to Kalem Luga, c/o a business office in Dubai. An obliging concierge promised to post it for him, right away, priority mail.

Hostile Takeover

The Hunter panned his mini video recorder across the driveway and let it rest on the bushy hedge on the side of the gate. Then he slowly zoomed in on a spot on the ground underneath the hedge. He switched the recorder off and sat watching the buildings beyond the gate for a while. The business sign was clearly visible from where he had pulled off the side of the Rockcliffe Parkway. Bald Eagle Air Transportation Inc. It even had a childishly-rendered stylized logo, which he guessed was a bald eagle. It was nothing like the beautiful, powerful and mystical double-headed eagle that featured so proudly on the Albanian flag. With a sigh, he started up the Tucson and drove off.

He returned periodically through the day, sometimes driving slowly by, often stopping for a short period to observe. He could see that the security was good. There were no cameras, but he had spotted a number of electronic warning devices outside. He had no doubt that these were linked up with the police. They must have been expecting trouble, he thought.

His opportunity came just after 3:00 p.m. A new Jeep Wrangler, Mountain Edition, with a Rescue Green paint job drove out of the gates with three women in it. The same company logo was emblazoned on both sides of the Jeep. It was a fair assumption that it carried three employees. The Hunter followed at a careful distance. The Jeep drove south, over the main highway system, to a series of big box retail stores arranged around a massive parking lot. The ladies parked their Jeep in the row directly outside one of the entrances, but chose a bay far away from the entrance itself. The Hunter smiled. He had given his son the same advice. Find a quiet spot to park in and your car would suffer fewer parking lot nicks and scratches.

The Hunter had no such issues. He backed into a nearer bay,

looking outward and waited. He got his mini recorder ready.

The three ladies came walking by and the Hunter videotaped them chatting and laughing on their way to the shopping center. There were two Chinese girls in their twenties or thirties. He had difficulty telling the age of orientals. They were being chaperoned by a western woman in her late fifties to early sixties. Just the right age to be the mother of one of his targets, he hoped.

The Hunter started his SUV and moved it to the same row, but chose a spot two bays further from the entrance than the Jeep. Here he fiddled with his GPS and made sure that it was set to go to his new address. Then he switched that off and pocketed it, together with the power cable.

As he waited, he kept his eyes moving, watching the entrance mainly, but also on the lookout for any other threats. He reflected on how easily he had found Hanson and Goode. It had taken him all of 30 seconds to google them on his laptop and to find the story of their emergency landing in the Ottawa Sun. The story gave him their ages, the name of their company and a photograph showing him what they looked like. It was barely a challenge. He had looked up Bald Eagle Air Transportation and in another minute had their address. He had studied this using google maps and made sure he understood all the routes around it. The satellite detail was surprisingly good, too.

In 30 minutes, the ladies came out of the center and headed for their car. One of the Chinese girls was pushing a shopping cart with a few grocery bags in it. They got close to their Jeep and the old woman pushed her remote and the lights flashed and the doors clicked. She opened the back door and the three of them started loading in the bags. At the end of this, one of the girls took the shopping cart to its collection point. The other two got into the Jeep, with the old lady driving and the girl behind her in the back seat.

The Hunter got out of the Tucson and moved quickly to the front passenger side door of the Jeep. He opened it, jumped in and grabbed the old woman's right wrist in one fluid movement. She had been clicking in her seatbelt and looked up with a surprised "Oh!"

The Hunter smoothly handcuffed her wrist and locked her to the steering wheel. He then extracted his Glock and pointed it at the shocked Chinese girl in the back seat. "Right hand, now!" he shouted. She blinked. "Now!" he repeated with his own empty hand out, waiting. She whimpered but put her hand out, closing her eyes, expecting the worst. The Hunter grabbed her wrist and handcuffed it to the old lady's headrest. "One sound and I will shoot you both," he said in a very believable tone of voice.

The other girl was on her way back now. She passed behind the Jeep and was on her way to the front passenger door. The Hunter simultaneously opened the door and slid out. The girl looked horrified and her hand sprang over her mouth. The Hunter grabbed her right hand, cuffed it, then opened the back door and pushed her in. She fought back a bit but was nowhere near strong enough. Once she was in, he clipped the open end of the cuff through the inside door handle. He closed the door and moved around to the other side of the Jeep. He pulled out his last pair of handcuffs and used these to secure the left wrist of the first Chinese girl to her side internal door handle. He slammed that shut, too.

When he got back into the front passenger seat he rearranged his prisoners in the back so that they were each cuffed to a door and their free hands were cuffed together. Then he turned his attention to the old lady. "Keys!" he demanded.

"They're in my handbag. Take anything. Take everything! Please, don't hurt us, especially not the girls."

The Hunter's reply was to slap her hard. Her dark glasses flew off, her eyes looked wild. "I want you to shut up. That is your only warning," he said calmly, staring hard at the three of them to make sure they got the message.

He found the old woman's handbag and dumped the contents in the floor-well in front of him. The keys were there and he picked them up. He kicked the rest of the handbag clutter around, inspecting it, then turned back to the girls. "Where are your phones?" he asked. They both eyed their jeans front pockets. He leaned in and fished them out roughly. These too went onto the floor between his feet.

Next he pulled out his own GPS and plugged it into the cigarette lighter socket. He set the unit up on the dashboard. "You will drive," he told the old lady, "And you will do it right or I will shoot these two and I will walk away. Do you understand? Take your time, I want you to know that you will be responsible for the lives of your friends in the back."

"Y-Yes, I understand," she said. She was still shocked from the slap.

"I will release your right hand. You will use the cuffs to secure your left hand to the door, through the handle. Do it now," he said as he opened her cuffs. She transferred these onto her left hand and managed to do as he had instructed without messing up. The Hunter jammed the key into its ignition slot and turned. The Jeep started. After a moment, the GPS went live and resumed its navigation to the address that the Hunter had given it. "Follow the driving instructions," said the Hunter. As they left the parking lot, the Hunter tossed all of the ladies' cellphones out his window and into a vacant lot.

The GPS took them south into a farming area that started alongside the highway to Montreal. It took them onto increasingly smaller roads further away from the highway until it reached the long driveway to an isolated farmhouse. "You have arrived," it declared. The Hunter pointed up the driveway and the old woman drove up to the house and stopped. She was shaking. The girls in the back were quietly sobbing. The Hunter turned off the ignition and pocketed the key.

"Out," he told the old woman. She climbed out, still tethered to the door and stood next to the car. The hunter got out, opened the back door and released the girl from the door handcuffs, pocketing these too. "Out," he told them both. They had to scramble together through the other side door, where they waited, tied together and tied to the door. The Hunter went around and unlocked the cuffs around the remaining doors. Then he cuffed the old lady to the other two in a human chain and pushed them all towards the small rectangular farmhouse.

The front door was open and he told them to go in, turn right, and get down the stairs. The stairs led to the basement. The basement was essentially an unfinished concrete box. The only non-concrete side was the roof, which was the wooden floor for the rest of the house. A line of six-by-six-inch posts ran along the center of the basement, holding up a main central beam which supported the ground floor above it. The Hunter took them to the center beam, and using the cuff still hanging off the first girl, fastened her to the old lady so that they were now secured in a circle around the beam. Then he disappeared up the stairs and the girls started crying a bit more freely.

The Hunter came back a few minutes later. He had a paper bag with the name of a pharmacy printed on it, and he was wearing rubber gloves. He set the bag on the floor and approached the old lady, grabbing her hand and pulling her and the other two hard against the post. He leaned down and pulled a sharp-looking kitchen paring knife out of his sock, stood up, and very precisely cut the old lady's baby finger off at the second knuckle. She screamed, more in surprise than pain. The pain would come later. She fainted as he put the finger into a plastic pill bottle that he took from his pocket. He extracted some antiseptic ointment from the bag, expertly applied it, covered it with some gauze and bound it all up in a crepe bandage. He did this while the girls, trying not to cry or vomit, looked on in horror, supporting the passed-out old lady between them.

The Hunter took the old lady's rings off her finger and put them into the same plastic pill bottle. Then he took the rings off the girls' hands and put these all into the bottle, too.

He left his gloves on as he drove back to the parking lot. He had used a towel to wipe down the Jeep for prints, but you could never be too sure.

When he got to the parking lot, he found a quiet spot and parked. He reached over and opened the gas can that he had wedged in the back seat. When he was ready, he pushed it over and the car filled with the smell of gasoline. He made sure that it fully drained and that the gas had pooled on both sides of the central drive shaft ridge. When he could see gasoline seeping forward into both of the front foot wells, he got out. He took his GPS unit with him. He left all the windows open, but before he walked away, he pulled what looked like a pen out of his top pocket, twisted it and dropped it into the Jeep.

The Hunter walked casually to his parked up Tucson, got in and drove out towards Rockcliffe.

After a 15-minute drive he pulled up to the front gate of the Bald Eagle Air Transportation company. He had already confirmed that there were no cameras pointing at him, so he dropped an envelope into the mail box. It was addressed to Hanson & Goode. He also leaned down and placed the pill bottle on the ground under the hedge. Then he drove back to the farm using the GPS since he still didn't know the best way to get there. The GPS took him on the highway past the shopping mall. Great eruptions of flame and smoke were shooting out of the parking lot, and fire trucks were racing across it, but anyone could see that they were far too late.

Open Communications

Ken was getting a little worried about Tina and the girls. He had called all of them and left messages on all their phones. Only Joy's phone had actually sounded like it was ringing, the others just went straight to voice mail.

When Simon and I got in later that afternoon, we found him quite agitated. While Ken was explaining to us what they had gone out for and how this could not possibly take four hours, I picked idly through the day's post. One envelope stood out. I opened it and found a DVD inside. There was no note attached or anything, which made it suddenly very suspicious.

"What's that?" Simon asked.

"I don't know. Let's try it. It was addressed to us," I said, opening the DVD drawer on Ken's desktop.

After a lot of whirring and clicking, a movie player came up. It needed a prompt to get it going. I clicked the "Play" icon and suddenly Detective Sergeant Parry came into the picture. He was lying down with his hands held over a block of some sort. Then we saw the handcuffs. I went cold. A voice from off camera said "Look up, Parry", which he did, then a hammer came out of nowhere and obliterated his finger. The screaming was terrible.

"For fuck's sake, turn it off!" shouted Simon. He'd gone white. I clicked the stop icon, nothing happened, the screaming continued until Parry obviously blacked out. Then we saw him being revived with water. The film had obviously been edited and it became apparent that Parry's suffering took place over a longer time than we were witnessing. When his already shattered finger was smashed again I had to run outside to puke.

I got back to hear Parry saying, "Eric Hanson and Simon Goode," then there was a bang and the screen suddenly had stuff all over it. We could still see Parry. His head now had a large hole in the side nearest the camera and the bits fouling the screen were obviously pieces of brain. It was disgusting. Sickening. Incredibly scary.

The movie continued, jumping to a scene in a car park. We could see Tina, Joy and Kelsey walking past looking happy and relaxed. Then it jumped to a page of written text. It took a while for us to start reading it, we were still in shock.

The text read, "Do exactly what you are told or they will suffer worse than Parry. No police."

Then the movie skipped to our front gate, zoomed in a little tighter onto our postbox, then zoomed very tight onto a spot below the hedge. It held there for a while then went dead.

"The fuckers!" exploded Ken. "I am going to *kill* those fuckers!" The way he said "kill," I really believed he would. However, the violence of what we had just seen left me in no doubt of who was really in charge right now.

We looked at each other, fearing the worst for the girls but not quite sure how to proceed. Simon said, "I'm going to check outside." He came back in three minutes, gagging, fuming and terrified all at once. "Look what these bastards left us!" he said, his eyes wide.

I grabbed it and turned it upside down on Ken's desk. I registered the clink of jewelry and I saw the blackened digit but all I heard was Ken's howl of anguish, frustration and fear.

Ken's phone rang. He answered it using the speakerphone. It was the OPP. They had been patrolling the highway when they noticed a car in flames in the shopping center parking lot. It wasn't really their beat, but they were right there, so they pulled in to make sure lives were not endangered. They couldn't get anywhere near the car, but they noted the plate number before it burned up. After the fire department had arrived and extinguished the blaze, they took a preliminary look inside. They saw no evidence of bodies, but they did get a sense that an accelerant has been used. It seemed to have been arson. So the OPP cops looked up the plate number and traced the car back to BEAT Inc.

Ken was still recovering from the movie and his shocked response must have sounded very authentic to the OPP officer. I heard him say, "Don't worry Sir, these things happen. It's usually the kids, unfortunately. Are you insured?"

He had to repeat the question to Ken, then left him to come to terms with the loss of the Jeep.

Contract Negotiation

The phone rang in Philadelphia and the member of the Organization picked it up. "Hello?" he said.

"Ah, I'm calling from Wolf in Canada. We have a little problem in Quebec that I would like to discuss."

"Okay, I will find your number and call you back," he said, and put the phone down.

A minute later the phone rang in the CEO's suite at Wolf Copper Resources' head office in Toronto. It was a private, unlisted number that only his very trusted contacts had. Everyone else had to go through his secretary. "Brannah," he answered.

"You called us in Philadelphia earlier, Mr. Brannah. How may we assist you?" asked a cultured voice.

"Thank you, yes," he cleared his throat. "I am concerned that we had an agreement, the obligations of which your side have not met. There is a certain gentleman, still living with his mother on their farm up in northern Quebec. The operative word here is "still". Our agreement had specified that this status was to be changed."

"We are working on this, Mr. Brannah. You might have heard that a previous attempt to, ah, change his status was thwarted. The good news is that we have an expert in the field, very close to the scene as we speak. His intervention success rate is excellent. I am very confident that you will be pleased with the outcome."

"Thank you. When can I expect the conditions of our agreement to be fulfilled?" asked Brannah.

"Oh, any day now. Good bye, Mr. Brannah. Thank you for your business." The voice hung up. Brannah stared out of his high elevation window, thinking.

~

The Hunter received a coded email from the Organization to call at his earliest convenience. He picked it up at the Starbucks. He closed down his laptop and went looking for a suitable pay phone. A call box was found on the sidewalk and he used it to call Philadelphia. The Organization told him that they would consider it a significant return favor if the Hunter would kill a Mr. Jacques du Rand of Summerview Farm, Randville, Quebec. An attempt had already been made and it had failed. The customer was getting edgy. *Gjahtar* had an excellent reputation in this respect, flattered the Organization member. By swiftly completing this outstanding job, he would endear *Gjahtar* to the Organization to the point of continued logistical and financial support for the duration of his adventures, even beyond this mission in Canada. Could he do it? It would only take a day or so to drive up there. The Hunter agreed, reluctantly. He did not need the distraction right now. Nevertheless, he did owe these folks for their generous assistance, so they chatted some more about the details, and then hung up.

Shotgun Clause

It was breakfast time the following morning and Ken was doing his best to provide the guests with the kind of meal they had grown to expect from Tina. It was nearly as good. The guests wanted to know where Tina and the girls were. Ken told them that they had won a surprise cruise to Jamaica, which had required that they go immediately. Although he had calmed down to a seething, helpless rage by then, the guests could see that he was not himself. They assumed that he was pissed off about having been left to do all the work while the girls partied it up in the Caribbean.

When it was over, Ken called us over to the office, Joe included. We told Joe what had happened the previous evening. We didn't show him the video. Nobody had the stomach for it.

"They want something," Ken stated. "These guys are pretty organized. They could have killed us easily by now. So why did they take Tina and the girls? They want something from us. Threatening the women ensures that we comply."

"What do you think it is?" asked Joe.

"Oh we'll know soon enough," Ken replied. "Look, I think we have to just keep going. Maintain our regular schedules. If anyone finds out what's up, it could be worse for Tina, Joy and Kelsey. We don't want any panic outcomes okay?" he looked at each of us in turn.

I could see that Ken was taking the lead because he believed he had more to lose, but in reality, the girls had become family, too. I felt awful that they might be getting tortured or raped on account of Simon and me.

Ken continued, "Guys, let's keep this thing strictly between us, okay? Seeing how those animals dealt with your policeman friend has me worried sick for Tina and the girls. Please, let's not fuck it up for them, all right?"

We all nodded.

"Okay, go do your thing today. Don't let this cloud your piloting judgment. Be safe. I'll try to figure out our best move from here and we'll chat again when you get home."

Ken received an email within an hour, but of course we had already left on our re-supply runs for the day. The email simply said, "Meet me where the car burned. Be there at 5:00 p.m. today." Ken got on the radio and asked Simon and I to return to base for another drop before 4:00 p.m. We got through our planned deliveries quicker than normal and were both back by 3:00 p.m. Ken showed us the email. I felt sick again.

"Any ideas how we do this, Ken? Do we want to involve the police? I'm sure they're good at this sort of thing," said Simon. I could see where his thoughts had led him today.

"Let's go listen to what they have to say. We can better evaluate how the cops might factor into this after the meeting," answered Ken. He was dead against police involvement, but I could see that he was trying to accommodate Simon as best as possible. The internal game was almost as important as the external one.

"So, is there anything that we should prepare for?" I asked Ken.

His view was that we go there to arrive just before 5:00 p.m. We shouldn't have anything on us that could cause the ladies any harm if found, so no weapons, recorders or anything like that. It was crystal clear to Ken that we would be coerced into doing something. The only question in his mind was what. He argued that we should ask for proof of life. We had no need to carry out anything if the ladies were already dead. This made sense.

At 4:40 p.m. we drove out of our gate in Ken's truck and made our way over to the big box shopping center. We pulled into the parking lot exactly 17 minutes later. It took another couple of minutes to locate the burned out shell of the Jeep. We pulled in next to it and got out.

The Jeep was barely recognizable. The metal roof had melted away. The tires were burned off the rims. The inside was completely gutted. We stared in horror at what must have been a massively hot fire.

"Not a pretty picture, is it?" came a voice from behind us. We started. "It's okay, you can turn around," he said congenially. We did. The man looking at us was about six foot two, about 200 pounds, about 45 years old, dark skinned but not overtly so. He looked fit. He had blue eyes which clashed rather strikingly with his short, dark hair. "Now as you know I have your womenfolk," he went on. "My colleagues will kill them in exactly," he looked at his watch, "twenty eight minutes." He paused menacingly, then said, "Unless I tell then not to."

"I want to know that my wife is alive!" blurted out Ken. The man looked at him for a long minute then put his hand into his pocket. I thought, oh shit, here we go! But he pulled out some harmless polaroids, which he held by the edge in a thin pack. He dropped these at Ken's feet. Ken bent and retrieved them, quickly shuffling through so we could all see. There was a picture each of Tina, Joy and Kelsey. A flash had been used, they all had red-eye. In each case they had their backs against a concrete wall, their hands cuffed together and holding today's newspaper with both hands on top of the page. The girls were crying. Tina was wincing in pain. Her lip was cut and her bandaged hand was swollen to twice it's normal size.

"She's in pain!" said Ken. His voice had gone flat and soft.

"Oh yes, a lot of pain," the man said. "Hungry too, probably cold, undoubtedly in need of sleep. She is going to get much worse, soon. We are going to hurt the others, too. Badly."

"What the fuck do you want?" cried Ken.

"Cooperation," he said. "Complete cooperation."

"Let's assume you have it," said Simon shakily. "What then?"

The man stared at him a while before answering, "You and Hanson will be taking a trip. Are your passports in order?"

We both replied with yes.

"Good. Pack casual clothes, for five days, for this sort of temperature," he indicated the climate around us. "Do that when you get back tonight. Make sure you are ready to go instantly. You will be told when. You will find out where at the airport. I shall accompany you. You will return alone, carrying something of great value to the people I represent. After you return I will authorize the release of the women. Any hiccups, any indiscretions, any attempts at heroism and they will suffer. Their pain will make Parry's pain look like soap opera."

He said this all so matter of factly, which made the threat so much more believable. He had already presented his cruelty credentials with the Parry video. We had every reason to believe that he would deliver as promised, perhaps even go the extra mile for us.

"You have our cooperation," Ken said. "Please, don't hurt the women any more."

The man simply stared at Ken and said nothing. Then he said, "In the meantime, we have some business to attend to up north. This will require your airplane. Have it ready to depart at 6:00 a.m. tomorrow with full tanks." He checked his watch; it was 20 after. Another ten minutes and the ladies die. "I have calls to make," said the man. "Go out the way you came, use the highway. When you approach the first overpass, flash your headlights three times to signal my man that I am safe and he should let you pass unharmed. Do not forget to do this! Go now!" He waited for Ken's truck to get moving and then walked away. We never did see where he went.

The Hunter walked into the shopping center to buy some groceries. It looked like he was going to have to keep those women alive for a few more days.

Competitive Analysis

On the drive back, we kept a sharp eye out for the first overpass. Ken flashed three long bursts at it with his headlights and we held our breath as we drove below it. Nothing happened, except the car in front of us sped up. I wondered about that. Could the bad guys have been right in front of us all the time, waiting to open fire if we didn't signal them in time?

"How many of them are there do you reckon, Ken?" I asked.

"I think it's likely to be at least three," he said. "The guy we met today, one at the place they're holding the women, and one roving, either following us, or as he suggested, waiting for some kind of signal somewhere."

"Or both," suggested Simon, making Ken involuntarily look into his rear view mirror. "This is messed up. But in a way, I'm quite relieved we know what they want now. It doesn't even sound particularly problematic."

"What, smuggling drugs?" I asked. "You don't think that's an issue?"

"Can't say if it's drugs or not," said Simon. "I hope it's not."

"Well, these are Albanians. I understand there's quite a drug trade going on with the Albanian mafia. Chances are pretty strong that we're being asked to mule drugs," I said more caustically than was necessary, so I added, "Sorry."

"Yeah, look I'm tense too," admitted Simon. "The thing is, we're going to do whatever they want us to, right? So we might as well believe it's not drugs."

Ken had been quiet a long time but now spoke up. "I've got bad news for you guys," he said.

"What?" I asked.

"You're going to die," he said, almost as casually as the mafia man earlier.

"What?" demanded Simon, incredulous.

"Listen to this," explained Ken. "I've been thinking about this for most of the day. The first thing that jumps out at me is the extent of the torture involved with Parry. Why did they do that? Why did they video tape it all? Remember, we only got an edited short of the whole thing."

"Well, what's your take on that?" Simon asked.

"I think it was done because Parry was seen to be the main culprit," said Ken, "and the man who ordered his death, probably Luga senior, wanted there to be pain. The second thing is the vigor they employed in getting Parry to tell them who else was there at the time of Luga junior's death. That sounds like a vendetta, like someone desperate to get even."

"OK," I said slowly. This was not sounding good.

"The third thing is the reason they purport to be exploiting you. Muling something? That would only make sense if you were going to mule the Cullinan diamond."

"The what diamond?" I asked.

"Figure of speech. Something of extreme value, but reasonably small, like a large diamond worth say ten million dollars, something like that," explained Ken.

"So, not drugs then?" I asked.

"No. The value is not high enough for the effort that they've put into this. There is no way you're going to Albania, especially not to carry drugs back here. It would be just as effective for them, and a whole lot less complicated for them, to simply grab somebody randomly off the street. They could use that person's parents or lovers just as effectively as leverage to squeeze them into muling drugs. Hell, they probably do that all the time.

"If you were going to go somewhere to pick up something of extreme value, then the destination would have to conform, like diamonds from the Congo or emeralds from Brazil." Ken was making an uncomfortable amount of sense.

"So you think we're going to be killed?" asked Simon.

"Yes. If it was me I would do exactly the same thing. Set your sights on some larger, imminent task, in this case your flight somewhere to carry something back," Ken explained. "Then I would give you a by-the-way job, in this case a quick fight north. Halfway to somewhere, I shoot you in the back of the head and jump out with a parachute. As an example, okay? Job done. You were never going on a long trip anywhere."

"Jesus, Ken, where do you get such grim insight?" I asked him.

"RIC," muttered Ken.

"What?" asked Simon leaning forward to hear him better.

"No matter. It's a long story," answered Ken bitterly.

"Jesus!" I said again. I was becoming quite the accomplished blasphemer.

"If my theory is correct, I can think of at least three confirmations that we can look out for tomorrow," Ken told us.

"One, he will arrive with a gun to shoot you with. Two, he will have a video recorder to catalog your pain and prove your demise to whoever sent him, probably Luga senior. Three, you find out that the destination for your long trip is supposedly Albania and that it's supposed purpose is for you to mule drugs. Or someplace equally banal, designed to keep you toeing the line."

The rest of the drive was made in silence.

Dry Hole

Tina looked over at Joy and Kelsey. They had quietened down a little and were lying curled against each other for comfort and warmth. Tina's finger throbbed mercilessly, pain unrelenting. She was grateful for one thing, though, and that was that their kidnapper had not cuffed them together around the beam again after he had taken the photographs. It had allowed her to cradle her painful hand against her chest and to lie on her side.

A bag of groceries had been thrown down the stairs at some point in the night. It contained six oranges, a pre-packaged sandwich each, a bottle of water each, and a blister pack of extra strength Advil. Tina had cautioned the girls to eat the food as slowly as they could, try to stretch it out until the kidnapper brought more. She had no idea how frequently they would be fed. So far the statistics favored something like once a day.

Joy peeled Tina an orange and Kelsey had opened her sandwich package. Tina would never have been able to do either with her hand as it was. Then they helped her with some Advil and a swallow of water.

They lay quietly, not daring to disturb the man above them lest he take it out on them in some cruel way.

At some time close to five in the morning, they heard the floorboards above them creaking as the kidnapper moved about. They heard a shower draining for a while, more moving and shuffling then the bang of a door closing. It was quiet enough that they could here the car starting up outside.

"Hey girls," said Tina, "I think he's gone for a while. Let's use the opportunity to look around."

Their eyes were as accustomed to the dark as they were ever

going to get, yet it was still dark enough that they had to feel their way around. They made their way to the stairs and climbed carefully to the top. It was a tiny bit lighter here, enough to see that the door was made of solid wood.

Just then, the front door banged open again. They rushed down the stairs and pretended to be asleep when the basement door was thrown open and light flooded in. The kidnapper came down the stairs, pausing near the top to turn on a light. Tina noticed where the switch was located. The man had a newspaper in one hand and his polaroid in the other. "Against the wall!" he commanded with no preamble whatsoever.

He took pictures of the girls first. Tina saw that the headline read something about Canadian agriculture. She took note of where the word "agriculture" appeared, it was off center on the right of the page. When it was her turn to get photographed, she fussed about trying to grip the newspaper with her sore hand and ended up holding it with her hands directly above the word agriculture, with her left hand index finger pointing subtly down at it. At the last second before the flash, she arched her one eyebrow. She hoped the kidnapper didn't think much of this. She also hoped that this clue would somehow help Ken.

The man left in a hurry, slamming the front door behind him. Tina went back up the stairs and turned on the light. Amazing what a difference that made, she thought. Then they set about trying to figure a way out. It seemed impossible, but she didn't want the girls to lose hope.

Trojan Horse

The four of us had spent the evening devising a plan. Joe was
an integral part of this. He volunteered to come along, hiding in
the luggage compartment behind the back bulkhead. He would
have Ken's 9mm pistol with him. If the killer needed killing,
Simon would dive the aircraft then bring it back up again. At
this signal, Joe would know to shoot him as soon as he could.

Our stand-down signal was a steep bank to the right followed
immediately by a steep bank to the left. We would find a
reason to justify either maneuver if required.

This meant we had to make a place to hide Joe. Fortunately, he
was a compact build. Ken worked most of the night to build a
false floor for the luggage space. The bulkhead had an oval
opening in it, usually closed by a cloth curtain and which you
would ordinarily step through to access this area. The bottom
of the oval was 18 inches off the aircraft floor. Ken's idea was
to build a second floor inside this compartment flush with the
bottom of the opening. This would create a hiding space for Joe
below it. The floor would be made with light but sturdy
plywood sections that could be pushed up from below for Joe
to get out.

I hemmed the curtains to their new length using Tina's sewing
machine. It wasn't a great job, but it was functional. Then I
ironed them to look as if the sharp bottom crease had always
been there.

Our hope was that the killer would fling open the curtains, see
that the luggage area was empty, and move on, letting the
curtains fall back over the oval opening. Then Joe could get out
unnoticed once we were in flight and making enough engine
noise to cover him. He would hopefully be ready for action
once Simon gave him the signal.

Joe practiced this twice at 1:00 a.m., then got to bed for a few hours of sleep. Sleep was fitful for us all.

The killer came for us at 6:15 a.m. He rang the gate bell and drove right in and parked out of the way under a tree. As the gate was closing, he got out of his car, locking and alarming it. He had a bush jacket on against the early morning chill. It seemed to me that a number of the pockets were bulging. He walked right into the office where Ken waited with Simon and I and said, mainly to Ken, "Just so you know, my car alarm is connected to a mobile phone. If the alarm is activated for any reason, even a clap of thunder, they all die." With that, he dropped the new polaroids on the table. "Let's go," he said, mainly to us this time.

We walked ahead of him to the Otter. We had taken the precaution of moving the chartered Otters to the airport in case he switched planes on us. Our Otter was still out of the water and the killer took his time taking a good look around it. If he didn't know what he was looking for, it was not apparent to us. Finally he said, "Put it in the water." We did. When it was in the water and sitting between the guides, he got in and started looking around. One of the first places he looked was behind the luggage curtain. My heart stopped beating. He noticed the floor height difference right away, and as he did he pulled out his pistol. He tapped his pistol against both on the bulkhead and the new floor. "What's in here?" he demanded.

"Control cables, flotation," said Simon, "It's built up to be used as an additional stretcher base. This used to be an air ambulance."

His off-the-cuff answer satisfied the killer. After all, Ken went to a lot of trouble to scuff up the floor and make it look like it had been there a long time.

The killer went forward and checked out the cockpit. After a

while he called out, "Get in here, let's go." I pulled out a seat
for him about halfway along the cabin. Not too close to us or to
Joe.

On my way forward to take my co-pilot seat, he stopped me
and dug in his pockets, looking for something. I looked down
and saw that one of his pockets had gaped open, and clearly
revealing a small video recorder in there. He found what he
was looking for. It was a scrap of paper with some coordinates
written on it. "Set your GPS for that," he commanded me. I
half saluted and moved forward.

Simon initiated the start. As I busied myself programming the
GPS, I said to Simon through the headsets, "We're in shit. He's
got a gun and I saw a video recorder in his pocket. That's two
out of three of Ken's confirmations. I doubt he's also going to
volunteer that he's taking us to Albania, he's not really the
talkative type. Let's just put him away ASAP."

"You're forgetting something. What about the girls? And
Tina?" Responded Simon. We really were in an impossible
moral position.

We flew north silently, lost in our own thoughts and struggling
to think our way out of this situation. Once we passed the
halfway point, I noticed that the GPS map had scrolled around
to reveal our destination as the Randville airstrip. Suddenly
Simon dived, then recovered altitude. He seemed to have come
to a conclusion. Well, I wasn't going to argue with him about it.
I turned around in my seat and said to the killer, "Sorry, birds.
We had to duck." He had been halfway out of his seat with his
gun in his hand. He stopped and sat back down. Just then, in
my peripheral vision, I saw Joe peeping out from behind the
curtain, so I continued the conversation to distract the killer.
"There's a lot of water around here. Plenty of geese make their
homes here and during the migration season..." which is as far
as I needed to go because Joe had knocked him out with a

whopping blow to the side of his head with Ken's gun.

I sprang up, telling Simon, "We got him!" Simon turned and looked at him for a while, then continued on his northward track. Joe retrieved the zip ties and rope that we had hidden below the false bottom and between us we bound him up pretty good. I left Joe covering him with Ken's gun and made an inventory of all the stuff in the killer's pockets. There was no giveaway address where they might have been holding the girls, no telephone. How did he get hold of his team members, I wondered? His wallet held only cash, no ID whatsoever, and no clues as to where he was staying. I looked into his video recorder. The card had been freshly formatted. Nothing there, either.

We phoned Ken to let him know that we had taken down the killer and he was in custody. Simon was concerned that somehow the rest of the killer's team might know something was up if we turned back suddenly, so we were continuing on to Randville, our destination. We told Ken not to involve the police just yet. We would squeeze the killer for information when he woke up. Then I called Jacques du Rand and asked him to meet us at his airstrip in 45 minutes. With Joe keeping his eye firmly on the unconscious killer, Simon and I had a heart to heart chat over the cockpit headsets. This was going to get messy.

Push-back

Jacques was waiting for us at the Randville strip. We transferred the still comatose killer into his truck. Joe jumped in the back with the gun and Simon and I climbed in front. We briefed Jacques on our situation and asked if we could use his barn. He agreed.

By the time the killer woke up, we had him in Jacques' barn, sitting in a heavy old metal patio chair with his feet and knees zip-tied to the sturdy metal legs, his wrists and elbows zip-tied to the armrests, and the fingers of his right hand individually zip-tied hard against the solid metal armrest overhang. The rope we had brought from the Otter had been used to bind him to the back of the chair around his midriff. This guy was going nowhere.

Jacques had instructed the driver to take his mother to see a friend.

After a while, the killer moved. His head obviously hurt and he reflexively tried to feel for damage. When his arm wouldn't go there he opened his eyes to investigate the problem. He looked around, confused.

"Okay, let's see what we got here," said Simon and threw a bucket of water into his face. This shocked the killer back to full functionality. He blinked and sputtered, coughing and spitting the water out of his mouth and lungs. We watched him recover.

I picked up Jacques' four pound hammer and waved it in the killer's face. "Recognize this?" I asked him sweetly.

The Hunter knew he was finished then. He quickly processed that his best option was to tell the truth. This way he would avoid unnecessary pain. And preserve his limbs. Although the odds were heavily against it, he couldn't exclude the possibility of escape, either. Or release. He needed to trust his instincts, so he nodded rapidly and said, "I will tell you what you wish to know."

It couldn't be that easy, surely, I asked myself? Simon arched his eyebrow at me, so I continued, "Where are the women you kidnapped?"

"Petersen Farm, 1215 Route 150, Ottawa, off the 417 to Montreal. They are in the basement, alive," he replied.

"How many men are guarding them?" I demanded.

"None. I work alone," he replied with a slight smile. Simon ran off to the house to call Ken.

When I looked again, I found the killer was staring hard at Jacques "I know you," he told Jacques.

"What?" said Jacques, surprised.

"You are Jacques du Rand. You live with your mother on Summerview Farm in Randville. Is that where we are now?" he asked.

My mouth dropped open. So did Jacques'. "How the hell did you know that?" demanded Jacques.

"I was coming to kill you today," he replied quietly.

"What the fuck! Why?" shouted Jacques. He grabbed the hammer from me and moved in on the killer, raising it threateningly.

"Wait!" said the killer sharply, just as Simon joined us again. "I told you I would tell you everything. I do not mind giving pain, but I do not wish to suffer. I do not mind dying, but I do not wish to be incarcerated. My current situation is hopeless," he indicated his captured state with his chin, "so I am going to tell you everything and then you are either going to let me go, or you are going to shoot me. Agreed?"

None of us had an answer for that, so addressing Jacques, he carried on, "The Albanian Mafia have expanded into America. There they are known there as The Organization. They helped me capture Parry and disposed of his body afterward. They found me the car and the gun and they leased the farm in Ottawa. I owed them something. They have an important customer who wants you dead, so we agreed that this would be my repayment to The Organization."

"Jesus!" I said. "Who's their customer? Do you know?"

He shook his head. "I only know that my contact laughed about the Hunter working for the Wolf. I am known as *Gjahtar*, the Hunter. I guess the client is known as *Ujk*, the Wolf."

"Wolf Copper Resources." I said to Jacques and Simon. "Bastards!"

"Well, at least I know now," said Jacques. "I wasn't expecting this to be about me today. This is an unwelcome bonus." Then, turning to the Hunter he asked, "Is there any way that you can think of that would help me identify this Wolf?"

"The Organization obviously knows who it is, but I only have a telephone number for them. I don't know anyone there." He recited the number from memory.

"What about us?" I asked.

"You were going to go to Albania, to be killed very painfully, worse than Parry, probably."

"Who by?" Simon asked.

"Kalem Luga. The father of Egon Luga, the man you killed. Kalem is well-connected in Albania. He is also very cruel. And very upset that his younger son was murdered and that he was unable to attend the funeral. He wanted retribution. I was going to force you there by holding and threatening the women."

"Why did he wait so long to seek this retribution?" I wanted to know.

"Kalem was only recently released from prison in Europe. He wants very much to hurt you personally," replied the Hunter. This explained a lot to me.

"If you were working alone," asked Simon, "and you accompanied us to Albania, would the women have survived?"

"Probably not," admitted the Hunter. "I had no plans to return to Canada."

"Jesus!" I said again.

Simon walked over to the workbench with his head down, looking exhausted. He picked up the Hunter's little video recorder that we had set up earlier and turned it off with a click. He dropped this into his pocket. Then he walked over to the Hunter and stood in front of him with his arms crossed.

"You know, I'm grateful for your information, Mr. Hunter. But let's look at the situation realistically. You tortured and killed Detective Parry. He was a colleague of ours. We'd bonded with him." Simon was just getting warmed up. "Then you kidnapped our girlfriends and our partner's wife. You cut off her finger. Then you come here to kill our friend, Jacques du Rand today, forcing us to be your transport." Simon placed his foot on the Hunter's chair and leaned in toward him.

"Now," he continued, "you tell us not only were Eric and I going to die, but that we were going to die in a lot of pain. And you were going to leave the girls to die; probably letting them starve to death in some hole somewhere." Simon's voice pitch had steadily increased as he summarized the situation, part incredulous, part outraged.

"Now you would like us not to hurt you or send you to jail?" he hissed at the Hunter. "Well that does *not* work for me!" As he finished his last sentence Simon straightened up, grabbed the hammer out of a stunned Jacques' hand and brought it down from above his shoulder onto the middle finger of the Hunters right hand.

The finger erupted in a shower of blood, flesh and bone fragments as the four pound head drove towards the thick steel armrest. The Hunter screamed. It was long and terrible. I had to go outside, white-faced with shock.

I got myself under control and made myself go back into Jacques' barn. I walked up to Simon and took the hammer from him. I went up to the Hunter and stared at him for a long time, building my courage, kindling my rage. All the while he could see what I was up to and it made him thrash about, trying everything to get away. The stub of his shattered finger jerked around independently, as the broken nerve endings forced it into uncontrolled spasms. Then, quite deliberately, I lifted the hammer and brought it down with all my force on his right hand index finger.

I could feel the head of the hammer slow momentarily, as it blasted through the Hunter's finger, before stopping hard against the steel. His finger disappeared in a puff of red mist.

The Hunter's scream came from some primordial place. It was

part howl, part roar, part plea for death. I forced myself to watch the blood squirting from his hand in a wildly unrestrained double stream, until he passed out.

As the unconscious Hunter's chin hit his chest, there was a loud bang and a bullet tore a hole straight down into his brain. He twitched and stopped moving altogether. I whipped around to find Jacques holding Ken's smoking 9mm. "Sorry, guys, I think that was enough, don't you?" he asked reasonably.

Into the ensuing silence, Joe eventually said, with feeling, "*Fuck!* Remind me not to piss you people off!"

Exit Strategy

Joy and Kelsey heard the vehicle come to a skidding stop above them, outside. It frightened them. Why was he in such a hurry? Trembling, they shook Tina awake. As Tina slowly focused, pain coursing through her arm, Joy broke down in fearful tears. This set Kelsey off too. With both girls sobbing loudly, and Tina trying to softly console them, she almost missed Ken's anxious call from upstairs.

"Ken! Down here!" she shouted back, voice pitch rising as she pushed Joy and Kelsey off her to rush up the stairs. The girls wailed louder, as they followed urgently behind her.

Ken found them pounding on the basement door. They were scared, tired, hungry, and in Tina's case, in a lot of pain. But they were alive.

~

Jacques promised to dispose of the Hunter. There were many abandoned prospecting trenches in these parts, he informed us. It seemed fitting that this was where an assassin, hired by Wolf Copper Resources, would end up.

~

Joe, Simon and I flew back from Randville in near silence. Just after he made the final turn to line up with the Ottawa River, Simon turned to me and said through the headset, "You know that this doesn't end here, don't you?" I turned to look at him as he continued, "If Kalem Luga is this committed to revenge, you know that he won't stop now, right? We're going to be looking over our shoulders constantly now, until we kill him. Or he kills us."

I shivered.

www.ingramcontent.com/pod-product-compliance
Lightning Source LLC
Chambersburg PA
CBHW070621130626
46556CB00001B/432

* 9 7 8 0 9 8 6 6 9 4 4 1 7 *